Murder at the Residence

Murder at the Residence is first published in English
the United Kingdom in 2023 by Corylus Books Ltd,
and was originally published in Icelandic as
Morðið á Bessastöðum in 2012.

This book has been translated with a financial support from:

 **ICELANDIC LITERATURE CENTER**

Published by agreement with Forlagið
www.forlagid.is

Corylus Books Ltd

corylusbooks.com

ISBN: 978-1-7392989-2-0

Murder at the Residence

Stella Blómkvist

Translated by Quentin Bates

Published by Corylus Books Ltd

1

New Year's Eve 2009

The Year of the Crash has gone all the way to hell. Right back where it came from.

It's been three months since a syndicate of financial criminals and political gangsters flushed the economic wellbeing of our Icelandic nation down the toilet. That's after our award-winning export Vikings had already stripped bare the banks and most of the country's larger companies. Then they ran for it and stashed the loot in overseas tax havens – leaving the people of Iceland to pick up the tab. They'll be years paying that off; that's years of unemployment, taxed until we squeal. And let's not forget the extortionate interest rates. Then there's the welfare state being ground into the dust, and all under the watchful eye of the IMF.

Nobody's keen to take responsibility for this expensive chaos. All the same, this is manmade chaos.

The anger of the powerless erupts in increasingly frequent protests on Austurvöllur, right in front of the Parliament that's in the pocket of those behind the system. That's where the boys in black brought out batons, pepper spray and tear gas as they fought back against the protestors yesterday.

It's only going to get worse.

On the other hand, the financial collapse did nothing to

puncture New Year's firework frenzy. Those imported gunpowder cakes lit up the night sky over Reykjavík as never before, like a computer-choreographed blitz. Hundreds of millions of krónur went up in smoke in a short-lived orgasmic moment. Not that this was much more than small change in the screwed-up world of the fucked-up guys who bankrupted the country.

When I go downtown on New Year's Eve to get myself a helping of nightlife there are empty cartons strewn through the woods of Öskjuhlíð like smashed driftwood on a northern shore. This morass of half-burned firework packaging is the visible memorial to the last crazy convulsion of 2008. Yeah, that and the credit card bill. But nobody needs to worry about that until February or March. That's way off in the distant future.

The night's young. Bursting with tempting delights.

I put aside thinking about everyday priorities, my wonderful daughter and the Stella Fund. Instead, I'm focused on drinking and partying. For hours on end. All the way, until this long night of soaking-it-all-up comes to an end.

The beat of the fuck-me music that permeates the sad bars along Austurstræti has lost its magic. It's turned into a grating din that has my nerves shrieking in irritation.

I glance at my angular gold watch.

A Cartier Tank Americaine. That's the kind of watch that costs a cool million in a boutique in Paris. Or so Ludmilla said. That's my friend from Latvia. It could just as easily be a cheap imitation from Hong Kong or Singapore.

It's getting on for four in the morning.

Sheesh!

I've been through the old city of Reykjavík's fun palaces all night without getting a sniff of a chance to slake the lust smouldering inside me. The hunks are mostly too wasted. Floppy and boring. And the chicks are mostly focused on finding any serviceable guy who isn't hurtling towards bankruptcy.

To hell with it! Time to head home. Accept the cold reality of it.

Too old now to be hunting by night. Counting down to being sentenced to turn forty. In the middle of summer. That's just a few months away. It's like looking into an ice-cold black pit with no hope of escape.

I drain my glass. I let Jack Daniels linger on my tongue for a moment. The Tennessee nectar.

Ah.

He's my old and trusted friend. The only one who's never let me down.

The toilets in this shabby boozer are down in the basement. The wooden steps creak with every footfall.

Four middle-aged guys lounging in front of a closed door. A queue of some kind. The youngest looks up expectantly.

'You do business?' he asks, a horny look in his eye.

'Sorry,' I reply.

The foreign guys watch me go into the ladies. There's lechery in their dark eyes. It's like they've been at sea, starved of feminine tenderness for the last three months. Or else somewhere high in the mountains with nothing but wind and rain for company. Screwing the perfect ideal of Iceland for the benefit of American minerals billionaires.

Two blondes in their twenties are hunched over the basins. One holds an open powder compact. The other has a striped straw in her hand. A little pile of something white rests on the compact's circular mirror.

'Want to buy?' one of them asks in English, looking up.

I shake my head.

The other one finishes snorting into one nostril. She wipes her nose with a white paper towel. She checks her dyed hair. Freshens up her pink lipstick.

'OK,' she says, nodding to her friend.

The mirror isn't as filthy as the basin.

It seemed right to be all in black tonight. I got my

designer to run up a black leather dress, Spice Girls style. She rustled up black boots that go half-way up my legs. Channelling Victoria.

I shake my long fair hair. My joy.

It's a light in the darkness.

The older blonde's negotiating with the three guys out in the corridor. They're right by the door as I come out of the ladies.

Two of them shift right away. They make themselves comfortable at the bottom of the stairs. Side by side. That blocks the way back to the bar. They're like a pair of self-appointed watchdogs.

Heavy orgasmic groans carry from the gents.

'Let me up the stairs, guys,' I say.

One of them spreads his arms wide.

'Come to daddy, baby,' he croons.

I try to push my way between the men. But they both grab. They're holding on tight.

The younger one says something in a language I don't understand. Just then, he slides a hand up my leg, over the top of one tall black boot.

His pal sniggers.

I glare into dark, drunken eyes.

'You want to go to prison?' I snap, in English.

'Me no prison,' the man replies, shaking his head.

'I'm a lawyer,' I continue in the same harsh tone. 'Hands off. Right now. Or I'll have you both charged with assault.'

'No fucking prison,' the guy repeats, reluctantly withdrawing his hand.

The other one does the same.

The blonde grabs my arm.

'You real lawyer?' she asks in stiff English.

'Of course.'

'Can I talk with you?'

'No. I'm going home.'

'Please. I'm desperate.'

There's anguish in her dark eyes.

'All right.'

Those horny-as-hell guys aren't going to let the blonde get away without getting what they've been waiting so long for. They encircle her. Their voices babble. Banknotes are waved. Euros and dollars.

She manages to calm them down. It looks like she's promised to come right back to deal with their needs.

I'm not going to interfere in private enterprise. Let alone meddle in every patriarchy's oldest profession. But these girls' enthusiasm for their work seems to be at a low ebb, if they need to pep themselves up with a blast of white powder between clients.

The girl follows me up the stairs. There are three of the boys in black in full uniform waiting at the top of the stairs. Two of them are young bucks. One's fair. The other has dark hair. The third is a red-haired girl. Looks hardly more than twenty.

'Do good business down there?' the fair-haired one asks in easy English, with a superior grin on his face.

'Has the police college stopped teaching youngsters manners?' I retort, my voice waspish.

The grin slips from the face of the boy in black.

'Show me your ID,' he orders.

'My name's Stella Blómkvist and I'm a lawyer,' I say coldly, handing him a business card. 'Come to my office if you need to talk to me.'

'Sorry,' the redhead interrupts. 'Glúmur mistook you for someone else.'

'What's your name?' I ask.

'Rósalind, and this is Eiríkur.'

Glúmur jostles his way past and down the stairs. Eiríkur follows right behind, like a faithful dog.

I look into Rósalind's eyes. They're a beautiful green – like flashes of beguiling emerald.

An old exclamation rises up from the depths of memory,

Oh, the delight that is Rósalind!

I wet my lips. It's instinctive.

'Pleased to meet you, Rósalind,' I smile. 'A shame you're on duty tonight.'

She smiles back awkwardly, looks away and hurries down the stairs behind her colleagues.

Nice!

It's too bad that she's not at a loose end. I could definitely talk her round. All the way to paradise. No question.

At the bar I order a glass of the dark brown Tennessee nectar. I let Jack Daniels tease my tonsils as I look this foreign girl up and down. She's young, too much make-up, dyed blonde, with pale pink lips and jaded eyes.

Dagnija's from Latvia. That's the homeland of my friend Ludmilla. She works at El Dorado. The city's most notorious strip joint owned by Sigvaldi Auðólfsson. Known as Porno Valdi.

She's worried sick about her friend. Ilona hasn't been seen for almost a week. She hasn't answered text messages. But nobody's looking for her. It's like nobody cares.

'Sigvaldi says Ilona met a good customer and she'll show up soon,' Dagnija says in her stilted English. 'But I know Ilona would have called me if everything was OK. We've been together since school, she's my best friend. Something bad's happened to her. I'm sure of it.'

I listen to the girl for a while. Then I pull a card from my little white handbag.

'We can't do anything in the middle of the night,' I say. 'Come to my office on Friday. If you haven't heard from your friend by then.'

'OK,' Dagnija says.

I call a cab. Make myself comfortable on the back seat. I stare through the windows at the hardcore night owls wandering the city centre. There's also the multi-coloured displays of salesmanship doing its utmost to persuade passers-by to buy the most ridiculous junk.

There's nobody home at my place. The red house with the white-framed windows and black roof that's both home and office. My daughter Sóley Árdís is in Álftanes. She's with Cora and her husband, who happens to be my cousin Sissi. Fast asleep by now.

I glug cold water from the kitchen tap. Sparkling clean Icelandic water combats booze-related dehydration. Much less chance of a hangover when the sun shows itself again. That was the most useful thing I learned in my first year at university. That came from a happily married lecturer in medical science. And I drank him into bed.

He was so proud of never getting a hangover.

I struggle to get to sleep, naked under the down-soft duvet. Even though the first morning of the year is about to dawn.

Images of the night flash through my mind. People and bars. The barmen who so deftly serve the sweet nectar. The music that changes in tone as the night passes into a coarse cacophony. The bottle blondes hoovering up coke in the toilets. The pushy fair-haired boy in black. And Rósalind.

Fingers find their own way between my legs. Searching out longed-for oblivion.

Sweet.

Those green eyes follow me into sleep.

2

Friday, 2ⁿᵈ January

The winter chill has taken a break.

It goes without saying that's just temporary. The Icelandic cold will definitely be back. Winter on the warpath. Frostier and more bitter than ever before. No doubt about it.

Lísa Björk is at work in the legal practice that occupies the whole of the ground floor of my house. I pull up outside at around eight-thirty in my stylish new silver steed, back from dropping my daughter off at nursery.

She hardly reaches my shoulder. Lísa Björk, that is. She's such a doll. Wide, deep eyes, plump lips and dark hair that falls in waves down her cheeks. She's a sexy girl with a sex phobia. She's never told me why.

I flip fast through the snail mail that Lísa Björk has left on my desk. One's from my mother.

She's written more often over the last couple of years. Since her only grandchild came into the world. She's even flown twice to Iceland just to play with my daughter. She's still doing her best to get me to bring my little bundle of joy to Florida.

Lísa Björk interrupts my reading.

'The Central Bank's in chaos,' she says.

'As if that's anything unusual,' I reply, my thoughts elsewhere. 'It's been a shambles for years.'

'No, I mean right now,' she explains. 'A group of protestors prevented the directors from going into work and there was a clash with the police, who used pepper spray and tear gas in the underground car park and in the lobby. Some of the protestors were hit by cars.'

Iceland's very own Ubu Roi symbolises the crash. The political king who gave Landsbanki to his party pals and his friends. Then bankrupted the Central Bank with worthless loans. All the same, he still occupies the throne of the money palace overlooking Arnarhóll. That's where the green statue of the country's first settler weeps in the morning chill.

It's no surprise that there's a harder edge to the protests against the imbeciles in power, who seem to have no idea where to turn next. The Foreign Minister demonstrating just how much he despised the protestors, who had spent weeks there on Austurvöllur, just added fuel to the fire of dissatisfaction. 'You're not the people,' he'd puffed. There's nothing like that unique blend of incompetence and arrogance to fuel the anger of people about to lose everything because of the crash.

I've never taken part in any political protest. I've been carefully vaccinated against mass movements of every kind. Always go my own way. Alone and unsupported. Free and independent.

'The El Dorado girl is here,' Lísa Björk adds.

There's a completely everyday look to Dagnija, in contrast to when I met her in the basement of that bar on Austurstræti. Much less make-up. Dressed in dark jeans and a pink sweater with long sleeves. Black snow boots.

'So you haven't heard from your friend?' I ask.

'No. Nothing.'

'You're sure she didn't go back home? To Latvia?'

'Yeah. Sigvaldi has our passports. We can't leave without his permission.'

'So he's like a jailer?'

She looks back at me wearily, without answering the question.

'Anyway,' I continue. 'Tell me about your friend.'

Dagnija and Ilona grew up in the same apartment block in Bauska. It's a town of ten thousand people in the south of Latvia. Not far from the border with Lithuania.

They went to school together. Had good times together. They had a shared girlhood dream of making it big as models.

New Baltic Models International signed up the two sixteen-year-olds, promising them a glittering future in the fashion business. A year later they were sent to work in Sweden.

It didn't take long for them to find out they weren't modelling clothes. They were just showing off their bodies. Nude pictures and pole dancing joints.

By then it was too late to turn back. They were caught up in debt bondage to the criminals who owned and ran the agency.

But at least Dagnija and Ilona got to work together. They've mostly spent a few months here and there, dropping their clothes in strip clubs in Scandinavian cities. Mostly Copenhagen, Gothenburg and Malmö.

They sought solace in drugs. Ecstasy. Speed. Cocaine. Prostitution came next. To pay for the dope.

They've been sent to Reykjavík twice. Three months at a time. Both times they've entertained at Porno Valdi's strip joints. And then there are the private parties.

Dagnija takes a photo from her bag and puts it on the table.

It's Ilona. Taken a few years ago. Back in happier times. She has a cheerful smile that reaches all the way to her eyes.

'When did you last see Ilona?' I ask.

'Between Christmas and New Year,' Dagnija replies. 'Valdi sent her downtown to a private party. Ilona called me around eleven and said she was in a cool SUV going to that party, and that's the last I've heard from her.'

'Nothing for, what? Six days?'

'Six days, yes. She hasn't come back to the place we're staying.'

'You're in the same place?'

'Yes, Sigvaldi rents us a room.'

'I assume you've tried to call her?'

'Yeah. She's not answering her mobile. I've called her number again and again, every day, but it's always the same, no answer.'

'Where was this party?'

'I don't know.'

'You don't?' I ask in surprise. 'Didn't Sigvaldi say where she was going that night?'

'No. He won't tell me. He just says it'll be fine and Ilona will be home in a few days.'

'He knows where she is?'

'It sounds like it. But he still won't ask her to call me so I don't worry about her.'

'Strange.'

'Yes. I'm sure that if everything was OK, Ilona would have called or sent me a text. I'm certain of that because she always calls me when she's working solo, until now.'

I look deep into Dagnija's worried eyes. I've made a decision.

'All right. Go straight to Sigvaldi and tell him that he has to put you in touch with Ilona by this evening. Otherwise I'll go to the boys in black here in Reykjavík, register her as a missing person and demand they start searching for her right away.'

'OK.'

'Let me know how Sigvaldi reacts,' I say, handing her a card.

'Thank you for helping me. What do I owe you?'

'Nothing for now.'

There's a chance Dagnija's concerns are baseless, and maybe Ilona got lucky. Snatched hold of the golden goose when she saw an opportunity, something that offers a brighter future.

I've no reason to trust a word Porno Valdi has to say.

Sigvaldi Auðólfsson got his start as a political fixer. He had a talent for discreetly solving awkward problems. No less of a talent for dropping political opponents in the shit. Later on he played a leading part in Reykjavík's pornification. He still runs the city's biggest strip joints. On top of that, he has fingers in plenty of other business pies that wouldn't look good in the clear light of day. That's according to those who know. Not that the guardians of law and order have ever felt his collar.

The most poisonous vipers no longer hide in the grass, as Mother said.

3

Breakfast is two cups of ink-black, super-strength coffee. That's enough to shake up the brains cells. Shoves the head into gear.

'Do you have time to go up to the Landakot hospital?' Lísa Björk asks.

'What for?'

'I have a ward supervisor on the line,' she replies. 'She says there's an old man on his deathbed who's determined to speak to you.'

I grab hold of the phone. Listen to what the nurse has to say.

The man's name is Hákon Hákonarson. The same as the old king of Norway who turned Iceland into a colony back in dark medieval times. Old Hákon. The evil spirit that blighted the country, reborn eight hundred years later as Iceland's political king. A special Icelandic version of Ubu Roi. So say those with a belief in reincarnation.

'Hákon could go at any moment,' she says.

'Does he want to make a will, or what?'

'I don't know what Hákon has in mind, but he says his dying wish is to speak to Stella Blómkvist.'

Ooof!

It has to be bullshit. But I'll do it. It's not far.

The old guy mumbles in his hospital bed.

'What did you say?' I ask, leaning closer.

'Death says checkmate.'

He's not much more than skin hung on old bones. His skin is pale grey, stretched across bones that stick out as if all the meat has gone from them. His hair's grey and sparse. But there's life in his eyes. They're blue-green like the deep sea. A pair of twinkling stars in a body close to death.

'I've outsmarted death more than once,' he continues. 'And more than twice.'

His voice is faint, hardly more than a whisper.

'Now my battle's almost over and the doctors say I have at best a few days to tie up loose ends.'

Hákon has a drip in his arm that feeds him. A computer monitors his pulse that flickers at around fifty beats a minute. There's an oxygen mask hanging down on his chest and occasionally he feebly pushes it up to his dry, parted lips.

I put my russet-brown briefcase on the floor in front of the monitor.

'It's been a marathon and it's almost over. I'm not running away from death any longer. No point now.'

'The nurse said you had a final wish. What's that?'

'The sin of neglect weighs heavy on me.'

'Sin? Wouldn't you be better off with a priest?'

'Not that sort of sin,' Hákon says.

A middle-aged nurse looks in when he starts to cough. She makes the old man comfortable in his bed. She moistens his dry lips, passes a damp cloth over his pale grey forehead.

'There you go, Hákon. That's better, isn't it?' she clucks, without expecting a reply. Then she's gone back along the corridor. A merciful angel in human guise.

This place gives me the horrors. I swear to myself again that I'm not going to end my days here in death's waiting room. I try to get this visit over as soon as I can.

'So, what can I do for you?' I ask.

'Are you in a hurry as well?'

'Yes. Always.'

'I'd like to ask you to clear the way for me to complete a task I never had the energy to finish,' Hákon says.

'Let's hear it.'

'I've always found injustice hard to bear,' he continues, his voice weakening. 'It's been a hell of a burden sometimes because in this world there's so much that's unjust. There are evil people running everything, and I'm sad to say I was never any kind of a hero. I often felt bad over the injustices I witnessed, and mostly never did anything.'

'Mostly?'

'Except once.'

Hákon pulls at the oxygen mask with his right hand and presses it to his face. The hand shakes and trembles.

I look away, glance around for a chair. I pull a white stool up to the bed, and sit.

The old man's stable, for the time being.

'What happened that one time?' I ask with impatience.

'Come closer,' he whispers.

I'm on my feet, closer to the bed. I lean down to his face. Even though I feel sick at the foul smell of death that's coming from him.

'I had to do something,' he breathes.

'What did you do?'

'Killed a man or two.'

I'm taken uncomfortably by surprise. I'm not sure I heard him right.

'You killed a man or two?' I repeat.

'Aye. There were two of them.'

I straighten my back. Looking into his blue-green eyes. They look perfectly clear.

'Are you messing with me?' I ask coldly.

'No.'

This makes me shiver.

'I don't regret it in the least,' he whispers. 'I had to do it to save my child from a terrible fate.'

'What child?'

'I'm asking you to find my child.'

'What child are we talking about?'

'She was about a year old.'

'Who?'

'I don't know what her name is now,' Hákon whispers. 'She was christened Ásthildur. She was given a new name when she was adopted.'

'When was this?'

'Summer 1972.'

I quickly do the sum in my head.

'So now she'd be getting on for forty?'

'Ásthildur will be thirty-eight at the end of May. Her birthday's the 25th of May.'

'Why should I search out this woman?'

'I want my child to know the truth.'

'What truth?'

'The truth about her parents. The truth about Hjördís and me.'

Hákon's eyes flicker to one side, to the white table by the bed.

'Open the drawer.'

I pull the handle on the white cabinet. There's a brown cigar box held together with tough red tape.

'Take the box with you.'

'What for?'

'You have to find my child,' he whispers. 'You have to tell her the truth.'

'What truth?' I repeat.

Hákon stiffens. The machine at his side emits an alarming squeal. His right hand reaches out.

I put the oxygen mask over his mouth and nose. I don't let go until the middle-aged nurse hurries into the room.

'Wait outside,' she orders as she attends to the old man.

The stench of death follows me out into the corridor with its white walls. I wait there a while, until the nurse comes out.

'All over,' she says.

'You're certain?' I ask, stupidly. 'We were in the middle of talking.'

'He's gone.'

I go back to the room where Hákon Hákonarson lies motionless. The nurse has closed his eyes. She's put a strap under his chin to keep his mouth closed until the body stiffens.

The pale, clear face is like a mask in a deathly theatre.

Hákon Hákonarson isn't going to say anything more about what he neglected to do, or about the uselessness of the gods of justice that we all know about.

I hurry out into the fresh air with the brown cigar box tucked in my russet-brown briefcase. On the way I can't help thinking about the ugliness of death, or about the childish expectations some people seem to harbour that good and justice will prevail in a society of swindlers.

Justice is the Fata Morgana of optimism, as Mother said.

4

There are everyday tasks stacked up waiting for me, not least the problems of the Stella Fund that didn't emerge happily from the fallout of the financial crash.

Just the same, all that can wait while I check out the contents of the brown cigar box. Hákon Hákonarson's dying wish gets priority.

I tug at the red tape, and lift the lid.

There's an old photo at the top. It's a colour print, the size of a postcard. The woman in the picture could be in her twenties. The picture is dog-eared and the colours have begun to fade.

The woman is painting the gable end of a two-storey wooden house. The paint's blue.

She's high up on a heavy wooden ladder. She smiles down at the photographer, can of paint in one hand and broad brush in the other.

She's tied a red scarf around her head. No doubt that's to keep the paint out of her fair hair.

Someone has written in delicate script on the back of the photo.

Hjördís painting the house, summer 1970.

Hjördís? Didn't Hákon mention someone called Hjördís as being the mother of his child?

And what house is this?

There are four envelopes in the box, three white and one brown.

One envelope contains a short will. Hákon Hákonarson seems to have signed it on Christmas Day. The two witnesses are nurses.

Hákon names Ásthildur Ásvaldsdóttir as his legal heir. He states that I'm to execute his wishes. He did this a few days before I even knew of the old man's existence. He was clearly sure in his mind that I'd go along with what he wanted.

In the next envelope are three yellowing newspaper cuttings. They're all dated summer 1972.

The oldest is from *Morgunblaðið*. Beneath the headline is a picture of a burned-out ruin.

Two dead in house fire
An old timber-framed house at Jórunnarstaðir in Arnarfjörður burned to the ground the night before last. When police and fire crew arrived at the scene at dawn, the building had already collapsed but was still smouldering. Police located the bodies of two people in the ruins.

It's also stated that the authorities hadn't released the names of the deceased, and that the cause of the blaze was unknown.

Another clipping is from *Vísir*, detailing that the police in Bíldudalur had identified the pair who lost their lives in the fire. Along with the news item are pictures of two young men, practically identical.

The Jórunnarstaðir twins
Twin brothers Ásvaldur and Rögnvaldur Hermannsson, the sons of bank manager Hermann Rögnvaldsson, had been living at Jórunnarstaðir for around a year, along with Ásvaldur's wife Hjördís, and their one-year-old daughter. The mother and daughter were away, having medical treatment in Reykjavík during the weekend when the farmhouse burned to the ground.

That's Hjördís Eyjólfsdóttir. The woman in the photo. The one who painted the house.

The third item is about the outcome of the inquest into the cause of the fire.

Heater caused fire
Specialists at the Reykjavík Fire Brigade believe that an electric heater used to warm the living room at Jórunnarstaðir was the cause of the fire, Bíldudalur police chief Ragnar Jónsson said in an interview with Tíminn yesterday.

No mention of possible arson. Not a whisper about murder. Maybe Hákon was getting confused?

I put the clippings to one side, and open the third envelope.

This time it's a photocopy of a letter sent six years ago by Hákon Hákonarson to the District Commissioner in Patreksfjörður. It states that he is the father of Ásthildur Ásvaldsdóttir, born in Copenhagen on the 25th of May 1971, and registered as the child of Hjördís Eyjólfsdóttir and her husband Ásvaldur Hermannsson. After they both died in 1972, Ásthildur had been given up for adoption and given a new name.

In his letter, Hákon details his fruitless attempts over the last few years to have the secrecy concerning Ásthildur's new name lifted, and reiterates his request for an opportunity to undergo DNA testing to prove that he is her father.

The letter is accompanied by a stamped report from deCODE Iceland relating to the DNA testing Hákon had undergone. There's also the Commissioner's reply, refusing his request.

So, what's new?

The brown envelope is larger and bulkier, carefully sealed. *To my daughter Ásthildur*, it says on the outside, in Hákon's handwriting.

Is this the truth of it?

My instinct is to pass the buck on this one. At any rate, for the moment. It's not as if I'm short of things to do with my valuable time.

I write a quick letter to the District Commissioner in Reykjavík, as that's where Hákon Hákonarson had his legal residence when he died. I'm sending him the will, and an account of the old man's attempts to prove that Ásthildur is his natural child.

Over to you, big man.

I stuff the rest of the documents back in the brown cigar box, along with the dog-eared photo. The box goes at the bottom of the furthest filing cabinet in the office. It's there with the paperwork for the other near-hopeless cases waiting for a miracle to occur.

Dead men don't complain, as Mother said.

5

Gamblers don't come much stupider than drug mules.

It goes without saying that life is all about taking chances. You win some, you lose some, and all that. But mules aren't putting money on the table. They're gambling with their freedom.

That means years of freedom.

Some of them even run this risk more than once. That's about as clever as playing Russian roulette with two or three loaded chambers.

One bullet could be fatal. Two is madness. Three is suicide.

I've no desire to meet Robertas. But I need to see him to find out if this criminal, of his own accord, asked for me to represent him. And why.

This Lithuanian guy was arrested in Seyðisfjörður before Christmas. That was when unerring sniffer dogs found a load of illegal substances carefully hidden in his car, a newish BMW.

The head of the drug squad is adamant that the Lithuanian himself wrote my name on a sheet of paper, of his own accord, as if he knew me.

But Robertas has been in custody for three weeks, and only now comes up with my name? Why?

'You're certain you haven't met this man before?' Gunnbjörn Hannesson repeats, glaring at me.

The thickset drug squad chief suspects I'm up to something. No doubt about it.

I take a careful look at his passport, especially the picture of Robertas. He's twenty-nine. Born in Trakai in Lithuania.

'Well, I don't recognise this bastard,' I repeat, and drop the passport back on the desk.

'But he knows you. That's for certain, considering he had your name off pat,' he continues. 'You have to realise that we have to treat this as suspicious, considering the man's a mule for a major narcotics ring.'

'What you treat this as isn't my problem.'

The drug squad chief's in his forties. His brownish hair's starting to grey at the temples. There's a wintry look to his face. It's pale and weather-beaten.

'I'm asking because this Robertas, if that's his real name, appears to have been here before.'

Gunnbjörn starts to root through a stack of paperwork that occupies part of his desk here at the headquarters of the boys in black, just across from the square at Hlemmur.

'We found a picture of him in the database from the 18th of October last year,' he adds. 'This same man was a passenger on a flight from Copenhagen, but under a different name and passport. He seems to make a habit of playing fast and loose with the rules.'

The chief finally locates what he's looking for.

'Here he is,' Gunnbjörn says, handing me a printout from the Leifsstöð airport CCTV. There's no mistaking it's the same man. 'That time he called himself Valdas. You recognise him under that name?'

'No. I've never seen or met this man. I've no idea if his name's Robertas or Valdas, or Napoleon Bonaparte.'

'Sure?'

'Of course I am!'

The chief stares at me with a suspicious look on his face. But I can meet his eye without flinching. I've nothing to hide.

'You don't think it's odd that a foreign drug smuggler that you say you don't recognise should have memorised your name?' he asks after a pause.

I can't be dealing with this crap any longer. I tilt myself back in my chair. I stare out of the grimy window at the ugly as hell buses arriving at Hlemmur and leaving again. Not a word.

He'll have to settle for silent stalemate.

'So when do I get to meet our boy?' I ask after a long silence.

'The interpreter's coming at ten,' Gunnbjörn says, glancing at his watch. 'In a quarter of an hour.'

'Who is it?'

'Svanhvít Daníelsdóttir. She spent a few years in Lithuania and speaks the language well.'

'Is she a court-approved interpreter?'

'Yes.'

I don't know her. Haven't had much to do with Lithuanian villains up to now. That's even though a few from that part of the world have been collared in the last few years trying to smuggle hefty amounts of dope into the country. The routes are by air or using the *Norræna* ferry that comes every week from mainland Europe to Seyðisfjörður.

Gunnbjörn sends a young boy in black to accompany me to the interview room. There's a long, brownish conference table, with six uncomfortable chairs.

There's a new flatscreen on one wall. It's tethered to a digital camera.

I take a seat. The russet-brown briefcase is propped against one of the table legs. I kill time by looking up and down the young buck in black by the door.

'What's your name?' I ask.

'Bolli.'

I wet my lips. Give him a glimmer of a smile. Let him know with a lascivious look that I'd happily eat him up. Every bit of him.

This appetising young buck starts to shuffle in embarrassment by the door. His cheeks flush pink. But he doesn't look away. As if he's letting me know he'd have no objection to being eaten up.

It's Rósalind who comes suddenly to mind, with her green eyes and red hair.

Two sweet blackbirds. That'd be a hell of a sandwich.

My thoughts shoot back in time, to student days at Laugarvatn, and fun times with Gréta and Rocker Denni.

Tasty!

6

Two fine young lads bring Robertas into the interview room. They usher him to a seat at my side. Then they're gone.

My new client is of average height. His complexion's on the dark side – wavy black hair, deep blue eyes.

He glances to the side, and nods. He comes across as chilled. That's even after a few weeks of isolation at Litla-Hraun.

He's been through all this before.

Gunnbjörn takes a seat directly opposite the Lithuanian without saying a word to him. He flips back and forth through a grey folder.

Bolli's fiddling with the recorder just as the interpreter shows up.

'Hæ. I'm Svanhvít,' she says, extending a hand.

She's short and plump. Light brown hair falls straight past her cheeks. Her eyes are hidden behind dark glasses.

Svanhvít takes a seat beside the Lithuanian. She puts a notebook and pen on the table in front of her, and looks up at Gunnbjörn.

'All ready,' Bolli reports.

Gunnbjörn starts by trying to pin down what my new client's real name is. He waves his passport repeatedly in front of him.

'Robertas confirms this is his passport,' Svanhvít says.

Then the chief slaps another picture in front of the

Lithuanian. It's the customs database photo from the Leifsstöð airport in Keflavík.

'That's you as well, isn't it?' he growls.

Robertas lifts an eyebrow. Then he shrugs. It's like he doesn't understand what Gunnbjörn is driving at.

After a lengthy tussle, he admits that he came to Iceland as a tourist last October. That time he used a name that wasn't his own.

How come?

His explanation is that he suddenly wanted to travel to Iceland. But didn't have time to get a passport. So his friend Valdas lent him his passport.

'You think anyone believes this bullshit?' Gunnbjörn asks.

Robertas thinks it over. He scowls. No answer.

'Telling us lies isn't going to do him any good,' the chief says, glancing over at me.

'As I haven't had an opportunity to speak privately to this new client of mine, I know nothing about him,' I retort. 'Or about this case.'

'We're expecting information from the police in Kaunas tomorrow or the next day, and then we'll be sure,' Gunnbjörn says. 'It would be a good move for your client to tell us the entire truth without messing around.'

Once Svanhvít has translated our conversation for his benefit, he repeats that Robertas is his real name and all the information in the passport is correct.

'Who sent you to Iceland?' the chief asks.

'I'm just a tourist,' Robertas replies.

'Who sent you?'

'Nobody sent me.'

'We found a plastic insert hidden in your car's tank,' Gunnbjörn continues. 'Containing illegal narcotics.'

'I know nothing about that.'

'Is this your car?'

'No,' the Lithuanian says. 'It's not my car.'

'Who's the owner?'

'I don't know.'

'So you don't know who owns the car you drove onto the ferry in Denmark and off in Seyðisfjörður?'

'No. I was supposed to be paid for bringing the car to Iceland. That's all I know.'

'For...?

Robertas embarks on a long explanation of why he came to Iceland in a car that's not his. He met a man in a bar in Kaunas. This guy offered him eight thousand euros if he'd take a BMW to Iceland. He was supposed to leave the car in Reykjavík and take a flight back to Kaunas from Keflavík.

'He gave me the keys and four thousand, and said I'd get the rest of the money when I get home to Lithuania,' he says.

'But there's no flight ticket among your things.'

'I was supposed to buy that myself in Reykjavík.'

'You didn't think there was anything suspicious about this offer?' Gunnbjörn asks.

'No. The man said he had sold the car to someone in Reykjavík and needed to get it to him,' Robertas replies. 'I liked the idea of being paid to travel to Iceland. In any case, I don't have a job at the moment.'

The chief digs deeper to get a description of the car's supposed owner. But my client's answers are so unclear that he doesn't get far.

'Nobody can take this bullshit seriously,' the chief says finally.

Robertas shrugs.

'Who were you supposed to meet here in Iceland?' Gunnbjörn probes.

'Nobody. I know nobody in Iceland.'

'Who was supposed to take delivery of the car?'

'I was told to leave in it a car park.'

'Which car park?'

'At the hotel.'

'Which hotel?'

'Hotel Grand.'

'Did you have a room booked there?'

'No. I was told to just leave the car parked there.'

'What about the keys?'

'I was told to leave the car locked at Hotel Grand and throw the keys into the sea.'

The drug squad supremo slams shut his folder. He glares at Robertas. His head shakes in disappointment. It's a way of saying that he considers everything my client has said is complete garbage.

'Who gave you the name of this lawyer?' he asks at last, jerking his head in my direction.

'He heard her name mentioned on the way,' Svanhvít says, after listening to what Robertas has to say.

'How so?'

'There was a conversation about Icelandic lawyers in the restaurant on board *Norræna*, and someone mentioned her name.'

'In what language?'

'The conversation was in English.'

'But the accused states that he doesn't speak English?'

'Robertas can understand some English but doesn't speak the language.'

Gunnbjörn wrinkles his nose. There's no mistaking his irritation.

'I would urge your client to be more co-operative,' he says. 'Otherwise there's going to be a long stay in Litla-Hraun ahead of him.'

'I'm going to need an interpreter so I can speak to him in private.'

'Svanhvít is available.'

'She's your interpreter.'

'I've often translated confidential conversations between lawyers and their clients,' Svanhvít says.

'We would never expect a court translator to break confidentiality,' the drug squad chief says drily.

'Then I want a few minutes with my client.'

When Bolli has switched off the recording equipment and followed Gunnbjörn out of the room, I turn to Robertas. I put him through the wringer, but don't get anything new out of him.

'Have it your own way,' I say in conclusion. 'It's your funeral.'

This seems to hit him hard. He looks from me to Svanhvít and back. Then he shrugs, one more time.

I get to my feet, picking up my russet-brown briefcase.

'But he says he's innocent,' Svanhvít says. 'He had no idea there were drugs in the car.'

'Nobody's going to believe that. Not even Father Christmas.'

By the door, I turn.

'Who told you to come to me?' I ask.

Svanhvít translates.

'He says the man he met in a bar in Kaunas told him that if he got into trouble in Iceland he should get in touch with Stella Blómkvist.'

'What's this guy's name?'

'Sergei,' Robertas answers, glowering at me. 'Sergei.'

7

The sun's hanging in the sky, just above a dark bank of cloud lying low over the sea to the west. The long shadows of the tall buildings along the shoreline stretch out over the city like a giant troll's fingers.

I park my silver steed on the dock. Directly opposite is the island of Viðey. I look out over the sound at the white-topped mountains on the far side of Faxaflói.

Sergei belonged in the past.

Or so I thought.

Robertas's statement brings back memories of a bitter clash with Auðólfur Hreinsson, Porno Valdi's nephew.

Back then, Sergei was Ludmilla's guardian angel. He filled the role on behalf of the father she barely knew, or so she said.

She hinted that her father had been a cold-blooded Russian oligarch. He could even have been an out-and-out mafioso.

Had Sergei really sent Robertas to Iceland as a mule? With a stack of drugs? And given him my name?

I don't want to believe it.

All the same, there are other questions popping up in my mind – uncomfortable questions.

If Robertas is telling the truth, could Ludmilla also have some part in all that? My Latvian friend who had herself been a dancer at El Dorado back in the day?

She visits me occasionally, when she needs to quench the thirst for love that burns deep in her heart.

No. Hell, no.

I sweep aside all such thoughts. I hunch over the wheel of the sleek Merc, slipping the silver steed between the lanes along Sjávarbraut. Heading home to my legal practice. Time to delve into the Stella Fund's problems.

Iceland is a hell of a cold place when you've no cash.

It's late in the afternoon when I switch on my mobile, just before it's time to collect my ray of sunshine from nursery. I scroll quickly through the messages.

One's from Dagnija. I call her number twice and get the same result both times. This phone is offline.

Two messages are from Sigvaldi Auðólfsson. I leave them. But answer the phone when it rings a third time.

'Didn't you get my messages?' he demands truculently.

'What do you want?'

'I want you to keep away from my girls.'

'No fucking problem,' I retort. 'You just need to stop losing them.'

'You don't need to worry about Ilona,' he says, ice cold. 'She's disappeared for a week before now.'

'You know where she is?'

'That one knows how to sniff out a golden goose.'

'You know where she is?' I repeat.

'I know she left here in good company. I've no reason to be concerned about her.'

'Dagnija knows her better than anyone and she's concerned about what has happened to her friend.'

'She won't be doing that much longer,' Porno Valdi retorts.

'Meaning what?'

'Dagnija is on her way to Copenhagen.'

'What?' I snap.

'She's going to be showing the Danes all the delights she has to offer for the next few weeks.'

'You shipped her out of the country?'

'I've precious little say over when these girls come and go. Dagnija's contract is with New Baltic and they say they want her in Copenhagen.'

'That's fucking bullshit!'

'And before Dagnija left for the airport, she asked me to pass on to you to forget everything she told you.'

'I'm supposed to believe that?'

'She knows now that Ilona will show up when she's had enough.'

'Dagnija needs to tell me this herself.'

'She asked me to give you this message, and that's what I've done.'

Porno Valdi ends the call abruptly.

That miserable stinking wankstain!

I try again to call Dagnija's mobile, but no success.

Knowing the way he works, there's no doubt that Valdi has shut down her phone number. That means her phone will be out of use for evermore.

That evening I'm lying rather than sitting on the leather sofa in the living room with my precious daughter Sóley Árdís in my arms. The TV news is all about the clashes at the black money palace, where protesters wave placards challenging the governor of the Central Bank to resign.

A knot of people closes off the main door of the Central Bank and the access to the underground car park. All the same, two Land Cruisers and a black Audi push their way through the throng.

This triggers an even harsher altercation. A few of the protesters manage to shove their way into the car park behind the cars. Heavily armed boys in black follow them brandishing their spray cans. They yell out hysterically, each louder than the other, 'Tear gas! Tear gas!' At the same time their colleagues bundle anyone with a camera back out of the building.

When the clash is over, there are people weeping here and there on the hard asphalt outside the black walls of the bankrupt money mill. There's bitter pepper spray in their eyes.

On the news there's an interview with a spokesman for the cops, saying that they were restrained in their response, under the circumstances. There are also interviews with protestors who don't spare their vitriol when it comes to the vicious reactions of individual boys in black who seem to have lost control, lashing out with batons for no reason.

A teenage girl had been run over inside the car park. Her left arm was broken in the collision and both her legs are badly bruised.

'That crazy guy drove into me deliberately,' a livid Freyja Dögg Hrólfsdóttir rages, glaring into the camera. Her left arm's in a white sling. 'I stood in front of the car and we looked into each other's eyes, and then he put his foot down and ran me down.'

A newshound says that a senior Central Bank official called Bjarni Bjarnason had been at the wheel of the jeep. He states that Bjarni declined to be interviewed in response to the girl's accusations, but commented that the protestors were nothing but 'crazy communists.'

'It was like the bastard wanted to deliberately kill me,' Freyja Dögg says, pushing her long fair hair back from her chiselled face.

Hmm. Cool chick.

I can't stop thinking of Dagnija when I'm ready to sleep. Sóley Árdís is already in dreamland.

What should I do?

After thinking it over, I pick up my laptop, and write an email to the head office of Reykjavík's boys in black. I set out Dagnija's deep concerns about her friend who has not been seen for a whole week. I scan in a photo of Ilona. This goes with the message and a formal request to initiate immediately a missing person procedure for the girl from Latvia, and to look out for her during their routine patrols through the city.

A clear conscience is the best sleeping pill there is, as Mother said.

8

Saturday 3rd January

'More! More!'

In the highchair pushed up to the kitchen table, Sóley Árdís waves her hands and feet. Her attention is on the appetising slice of pizza I'm holding. There's no let up to her demands.

'More! More!'

She's even pushier than I am.

It's fantastic how quickly she's learned to look out for herself, to stick to her guns. She issues strident demands for whatever she desires. More and more.

Speaking for myself, I've been an ardent worshipper of Mammon for years. I've been shovelling gleaming gold into the Stella Fund, in a literal sense over the last few months. Results have been comforting. But I'm far from satisfied. Now I need to rebuild everything I lost to the Icelandic financial crooks. Some of them are free to walk the streets, despite their crimes. Most of them have high-tailed it to London or Luxembourg. That's where the financial criminals aren't short of friends.

I was way too late figuring out how deep the rot went in Iceland's banks. There are plenty of us who came out of that badly. All I saw was what I wanted to see – the hefty dividends from my shares. Right up to the moment they became worthless.

'More! More!'

I get a kick out of dressing her. A lovely pink and red snowsuit, her hat in all kinds of colours, cute socks and neat little shoes.

My mobile buzzing dispels those warm feelings.

I instinctively check the number. I always do when it rings. Withheld number. I hit the red button without a qualm.

A minute later the phone's ringing again, still with no caller ID. I refuse the call again. I answer the third time it rings.

'Stella Blómkvist?'

The determined young voice sounds familiar. Not that I can exactly bring the voice's owner to mind.

'Yes.'

'You have to help me sue that bastard.'

Of course! The girl on the TV news. The one with the broken arm.

'And you are?' I ask, to make sure.

'Freyja Dögg Hrólfsdóttir. I was run over at the Central Bank. Didn't you see it on the news yesterday?'

She comes across as overwhelmed by her fifteen minutes of fame. She's just one more media star of the capricious moment. It goes without saying that it's as well to make the most of being in the spotlight – as long as it lasts.

'It's not a big deal. Did you get a document listing your injuries at A&E?'

'Of course. I know what I'm doing,' she replies brightly. 'And I have phone pictures showing that fucker running me over.'

'Send them to me.'

'OK.'

'Come to the office on Monday. Around ten.'

'OK.'

It's just below freezing outside. I button my thick white leather overcoat tightly about me before putting my little sweetheart in the child seat in the back.

We're on the way out to Álftanes.

My cousin Sissi and Cora are having their little boy christened early this morning in the church at Bessastaðir. That's where the President of Iceland rules the roost. Before it became the Presidential residence, this was where the Danish king's heavy-handed tax collectors lurked.

Sissi's wife Corazon – known to everyone simply as Cora – has thrived in Iceland, since I found her half-naked one night in the city. She'd fled a gang of Icelandic human traffickers.

She and Sissi clicked. They set up a digital services company that has been growing over the last few years. They bought themselves a place out on Álftanes with a view of the mysterious Snæfellsnes icecap across the bay.

They're waiting in the car park on the north side of the church. There are a few other guests there as Sóley Árdís and I pull up in the yard at Bessastaðir.

'The Reverend Jóhannes just called,' Cora says. 'He'll be right here.'

The hero of the hour is asleep in a pale blue carrycot. It's as if he's not excited at all about today. But he's at that enviable age when life is all about having enough to eat and drink – and sleeping, untroubled by trolls.

Sissi decided that the christening should take place in the old stone church at Bessastaðir.

'I really wanted a church that has a long and interesting history,' he says, his left hand clutching at his dark goatee. 'This one was built more than two hundred years ago and its walls are as thick as those of a mediaeval castle in Europe.'

'Is that right?'

'Yes, they're at least a metre thick,' he continues, failing to notice my sardonic tone. 'The stone was fetched from the lava field just to the south of here. The Gallows Field.'

'You know why it's called the Gallows Field?'

An awkward look appears on Sissi's face.

'Well, some criminals were hanged out there in the lava field back in the old days,' he says haltingly.

'Probably for stealing a length of twine. Or a bit of fish to eat.'

Cora looks up.

'The priest is here,' she says, opening the car door.

Sunbeams break through the cloud and play over the bright colours of the stained glass windows as we follow the grey-haired man of God through the church doors.

'The altarpiece is by Muggur,' cousin Sissi mutters. 'Jesus healing the sick.'

The Reverend Jóhannes pauses before approaching the altar and looks at it with a worried expression. It's as if something has taken him by surprise.

'Is there a problem?' I ask.

'I don't understand,' he says. 'The candlesticks are all missing.'

The parish priest steps closer to the altar. He stops before the altar rail.

'Someone has dropped vestments and a surplice on the floor by the altar,' he continues with a note of sadness in his voice.

I place my little sweetheart on the front pew next to Cora. Then I march up to the altar. I survey with astonishment the pile of clothing that occupies the narrow space between the altar and the rail, black and white clothing of different kinds.

'I fear that undesirable people have been here,' the man of God adds.

'We won't let it affect the christening,' I say with determination.

'No, not at all.'

I lean forward and tug at the black vestment that's closest to me.

'Hell!'

I find myself standing transfixed for a good while at the

altar rail. I stare down at the battered head of the corpse that has been hidden under the vestments. This is right below the painting of the miracle worker.

Jóhannes is next to me and gasps.

The body is that of an older man wearing an expensive suit. His dark blue silk tie is soaked through with blood.

I gesture to Sissi, Cora and Sóley Árdís to keep back. I take a closer look at the bloody and beaten face. It's clear that someone beat the victim brutally, and with great force. The wound above the left ear opens into the man's brain.

I instinctively look up to the altarpiece. To the Redeemer healing the sick.

But I know perfectly well that even the most famous miracle worker of all isn't going to bring this guy back to life.

9

Sunday 4ᵗʰ January

Still in shock.

I woke in the night, wrenched from sleep, screaming. Again and again, every time, the terrifying face of the murdered man appeared in my thoughts. Those deep wounds to his head. The congealed blood staining him from forehead down to his chin. That torn nose. Lips burst. Those dead eyes, still half-open.

I made so much noise that Sóley Árdís woke up around five.

She clambered into my bed. My warm arms, soft words and gentle kisses comforted her until she fell asleep.

But the horror of what I had seen in the church at Bessastaðir kept me awake for the rest of the night.

The elderly parish priest reacted quickly when he took in the sight behind the altar rail. He told Sissi and Cora that the christening would have to be postponed. He ushered all of the guests out of the church, asking everyone to wait in their cars until the police arrived.

I did my best to comfort Cora, who had so been looking forward to this day. She had a horde of guests coming for the celebration afterwards. But she was so overwrought that she wouldn't be able to do anything. That's even though I had managed to prevent her from seeing the corpse.

As far as Cora was concerned, this awful event was a harbinger of what the future held for her son.

The smart lads and the boys in black flocked to Bessastaðir. They arrived in a convoy at top speed, with flashing lights and wailing sirens.

Armed to the teeth, the steroid guys of the Special Unit stood guard between the church and the Presidential residence at Bessastaðir, protecting the home of the country's leader. As if they really thought that the President of the republic were in danger.

I made Sóley Árdís comfortable in cousin Sissi's car when I saw fat Raggi getting out of one of the vehicles. The CID chief superintendent is a sort of pal of mine – sometimes.

He sent a scowl my way.

'What are you doing here?' he rasped.

'I found the body.'

Raggi thought for a moment.

'I'll speak to you in a bit,' he said at last, marching into the church in the wake of the white-overalled forensics team.

The boys in black noted down the names of the guests and the numbers of their cars, and then shooed them all away.

Meanwhile, Sissi and Cora put their heads together with the Reverend Jóhannes, who told them he'd managed to find another church where they could christen their firstborn Sigurjón Magnús.

Cora was overjoyed.

The murder in the church at Bessastaðir was naturally the lead news item on both TV channels. Understandable, as it's been a few centuries since there was last a murder at Bessastaðir. That's as far as we know. And the President was in residence that weekend.

The body is that of a well-known financier.

There had been plenty of talk about Benedikt Björgúlfsson

in the wake of the financial crash. That was mostly because of his close links with the chief executive of Kaupthing bank. This was the business that had made Benedikt a billionaire. But it also played a part in bankrupting the bank.

The newshounds tried to make as much as they could of the murder, but they had precious little to go on, other than the victim's controversial background. The sleuths stayed tight-lipped. They wouldn't even confirm how Benedikt had lost his life, or when.

Maybe they didn't know.

Despite the dearth of information, the newsmen took their positions by the road. They showed images of the armed Special Unit guys on guard by the church and the residence at Bessastaðir. They brayed on about the measures taken by the authorities, the location's colourful history and the likelihood of a much greater security presence around the President following the murder.

Máki called during the afternoon. He's an old newshound who's gone from one paper to another for years and these days he runs *News Blog*. It's a lively online forum, not to be missed by anyone who wants to keep abreast of what's going on behind the scenes.

'I hear you're the one who found Bensi's body?' he said, not bothering with a greeting.

'You knew Benedikt?' I retorted.

'Only professionally,' Máki replied. 'Tell me everything.'

I had nothing to hide. I gave him a short description of events. That evening I saw Máki had filed a story

Star Lawyer Found Body
'It was a terrible experience,' said Stella Blómkvist, the high-flying lawyer who found the body of financier Benedikt Björgúlfsson in the Bessastaðir church.

Máki posted another article about how Benedikt Björgúlfsson had become massively wealthy following the privatisation of the state-owned banks around 2000. And he traced the links between the deceased and powerful Independence Party figures.

He had dug out confirmation that Benedikt had been among a large group of guests at an afternoon reception held by the President at Bessastaðir the day before the body had been found. He floated the question of whether the murder could have been committed just as the champagne was flowing at the Bessastaðir residence.

While the coppers had practically nothing to say to the media about Benedikt's murder, they weren't so reticent about the growing influence of foreign crime gangs in Iceland. Just like at other times when they had collared some drugs mule from somewhere in the Baltic States.

Morgunblaðið's headline set the tone.

Lithuanians taking control of drug traffic

This outlined that dope made its way up here to the frozen north from all sorts of directions – via passenger air traffic from Europe, container ships that arrive from ports on both sides of the Atlantic, trawlers that sell their catch overseas, yachts that rock up along Iceland's coasts. And not least, via the *Norræna* car ferry that comes once a week from Denmark.

The paper quoted Gunnbjörn Hannesson as saying that gangs in Lithuania had recently been sending one mule after another carrying amphetamines, cocaine and ecstasy to Iceland. Sometimes the police and the customs were able to intercept these carriers and take the dope out of circulation, but many of them could be expected to make it through with their smuggled substances.

'Unfortunately, most of the mules we have arrested recently don't seem to know anything of any importance about the people behind this, either here or in Lithuania. These are largely poor, ill-informed pawns who can be sacrificed without endangering the business the kingpins are doing. Our experience is that mules generally don't represent a threat to either the freedom or the security of those who manage these crime rings.'

According to the drug squad chief, it's an uphill battle to get any information about the kingpins in Lithuania. The police there have neither the resources nor the manpower to take on a mafia on this scale that dominates drug trafficking across the Nordic region.

'Crime syndicates in Europe no longer have to worry about borders. The most knowledgeable of my colleagues in Scandinavia and at Europol see Iceland as an integral part of this collective northern European drug market that's run by criminal mafias in the Baltic States and Russia,' Gunnbjörn said in the interview.

It's the same old song about bad foreigners making every effort to destroy Iceland's innocence. But it's on the overblown side this time. Our own home-grown criminals have long been perfectly capable of shovelling illegal drugs into the country. Not that they haven't formed a few alliances along the way with European mafiosi.

The chief of the boys in black clearly has an agenda he wants to pursue – to frighten the politicians into funding his department more generously.

'Police in Iceland need to be equipped to take on foreign crime syndicates and their accomplices here,' Gunnbjörn's quoted as saying. 'We need more police officers, better equipment and new pre-emptive legal powers to cope with this serious threat.'

Pre-emptive powers is one of those Orwellian expressions that sound so innocent. The two words in themselves are harmless enough.

But put them together and this means giving the boys in black legal powers to spy on people. It's a licence to tap innocent individuals' phones and emails, to snoop into all their dealings with their families, colleagues, friends,

acquaintances and any like-minded people.
First the dubious foreigners.
Then tomorrow it'll be you and me.

10

Monday 5th January

The phone pictures Freyja Dögg has were taken by her friend.

They aren't great quality. The hand holding the phone jerks sometimes from side to side, or up and down. No doubt that's down to the altercation with the boys in black doing their level best to protect the imposing palace of money that looms over Arnarhóll.

Although the images are grainy, they show clearly the events in the entrance to the Central Bank's underground car park as the driver of the Land Cruiser drove over the girl.

I watch the sequence again and again, until it's practically imprinted on my memory.

It starts with Freyja Dögg standing not far from the car. The blackbirds try to hold her and the other protestors back from the jeep that inches closer to the car park's doors. The driver's face is indistinct behind the tinted windscreen. But the vehicle's registration is clearly visible more than once.

The jeep's motionless as Freyja Dögg suddenly breaks free of the group. For a moment she's standing right in front of it, waving her placard with its message in bright red letters, yelling at the driver. There's no more than a metre or two between them.

Two of the boys in black are heading for her, just as the jeep takes off. It crashes into her. She's thrown backwards by the impact and falls to the tarmac, lying partly beneath the front of the car.

The driver stops while two of the blackbirds take hold of the girl, haul her from under the jeep, pick her up and bundle her away to the side of the car.

I gaze for a while at the paused image showing the face of Freyja Dögg just as the guardians of law and order take firm hold of her arm. She's clearly in great pain. She's screaming, not just in anger, but in agony.

Was her arm broken by the collision? Or the coppers' heavy-handed treatment? This is one of the questions that will need to have a definite answer before I can prepare a criminal charge.

Freyja Dögg arrives at ten.

She's in black from top to toe. Knee-high boots, jeans, a coat draped over her shoulders and a baseball cap over her long fair hair.

But the sling supporting her left arm is white.

She shows me the listing of her injuries by the doctor on duty at the National Hospital's accident and emergency reception. There's no doubt about it. There's a double fracture due to the force of the collision with the jeep.

I prepare a detailed criminal charge against the owner and driver of the jeep, Bjarni Bjarnason, director of the Central Bank.

Then I listen to Freyja Dögg's account of the protests she has been taking part in over the last few weeks. Her face is alive with passion as she describes the clashes with the boys in black who everywhere try to protect incompetent power-mongers.

'You're going to continue protesting?' I ask. 'With a broken arm?'

'Absolutely,' she replies. 'We won't let up until these corrupt bankers and politicians are out of power and preferably in prison. We need a new Iceland built on the wreck of the old one, and that's not going to happen without taking power into our own hands to clean up this lousy political system from top to bottom.'

Her passion is totally genuine. As is her innocent faith in being able to change the world by protesting against those in power. That's despite experience showing that the more things change at the heart of power, the more they stay the same.

We go together to the police station, in my powerful silver steed.

The guardians of law and order are nervous these days. That's the way it always is when the offices of justice are criticised for their servile support for political masters.

That means the capital's brood of blackbirds who have been stooping to increasingly harsh measures against furious protestors. Those are the betrayed Icelanders in their thousands crowded around the statue of Jón Sigurðsson on Austurvöllur. They throng around the hero of Iceland's struggle for freedom to demand that the country's government does something useful for those worst off, thanks to the recession triggered by the financial crash. Or that they resign and allow new people to step in as ministers to salvage what can be saved.

The boys in black are in no mood to accept Freyja Dögg's criminal charge against someone as highly-placed and powerful as the director of the Central Bank. But they don't have a choice.

Afterwards I give her a lift home. She lives in student accommodation on Eggertsgata.

'I didn't want to live at home any longer,' she says.

'How come?'

'They're both deep in this corruption shit,' she replied shortly.

'Let's hear it.'

She looks at me with astonished eyes.

48

'You don't know who my family are?'

'No. I'm your lawyer, not your parents'.'

'My mother is in Parliament for the Independence Party. Her name's Sandra Ósk.'

I see the connection.

'So you're Sandra's and Hrólfur's daughter? The managing director of what was Kaupthing bank?'

She sighs, and nods.

'Nobody chooses their parents,' I say in consolation as we part.

The black coat flaps like wings as she marches up the steps to the building. She turns at the door and looks back quickly. She waves with a smile on her lips.

Freyja Dögg brings back some emotions I'd prefer to let lie. She reminds me of myself in younger days that aren't coming back.

11

Hell!

That afternoon it's obvious that the blackbirds have done nothing to respond to my request for them to search for Ilona. That's the Latvian girl who was last in touch with her best friend before Christmas. That's nine days ago.

I'm livid. I rush out of the office without putting on a coat. Hurtle down to Hlemmur in the silver steed.

The inspector doesn't take kindly to me pointing out their failings when I march into their headquarters to ask why the hell they haven't done anything to find Ilona.

'We simply don't see this as urgent at this point,' Haraldur Haraldsson replies with clear hostility as he tilts himself back in his chair.

Arrogant bastard.

But he looks good in uniform. This guy's in good shape physically. And he doesn't mind showing it off. It's as if every time we meet he needs to prove his masculinity.

Sheesh!

'We've discussed this with Ilona's employer,' Haraldur continues. 'He assures us that this girl is staying with Icelandic friends and she'll surface soon enough.'

'Then it shouldn't be a problem to call her and get it confirmed,' I say.

'No. They want to be left in peace.'

'That's what Porno Valdi says, is it?'

'Sigvaldi Auðólfsson received a text message from Ilona

stating that she would return to work in mid-January, and that's good enough for me.'

'Did he show you this message?'

'He did.'

'When did it arrive?'

Haraldur turns to the computer on his desk. He calls up a document onto the long, flat screen.

'An SMS message reached Sigvaldi Auðólfsson's mobile phone on New Year's Day at 1846.'

'Last Thursday?'

'That's it.'

'How strange.'

'What is?'

'That Ilona should send Porno Valdi a message five days after she left for this mysterious party, without taking the opportunity to call her friend.'

'Most people are strange.'

'Has Sigvaldi heard from her since?'

'Not that he mentioned.'

'Where was Ilona when this message was sent?'

'I don't know that.'

'You haven't checked it out?'

Haraldur shakes his head.

'It's not difficult to get the phone provider to check it out.'

'We don't see grounds for this and the costs entailed,' he says. 'We've plenty to keep us busy right now. Society's in turmoil right now, as you may have noticed.'

What a shitbag.

'Is it certain that the message came from her phone?' I ask.

'Yes.'

'So you're telling me that Ilona has had her phone switched off for the last nine days, apart from a few minutes last Thursday? And that she made use of those minutes to text Porno Valdi and not her closest friend?'

'That's the way it looks,' Haraldur says dismissively.

'Why did she contact Valdi and not Dagnija?'

'Well, presumably because she works for Sigvaldi.'

'I'm not buying it,' I reply with a shake of the head. 'Dagnija is convinced that Ilona is in a bad way.'

'That's not what Sigvaldi says.'

'You don't think it's suspicious that Porno Valdi's reaction to Dagnija speaking to me was to ship her out of the country?'

Haraldur leans forward over the desk. He's obviously sick of arguing.

'We aren't going to waste valuable police time looking for a foreign stripper who's busy trying to nail down an Icelandic man,' he says with a cold grin.

I snatch up the russet-brown briefcase. On my feet in a second.

'If you are failing to do your duty, then I have no choice but to advertise in the media myself.'

'How you waste your money is no concern of mine,' Haraldur replies loftily.

I'm out of his office. I'm in such a rush along the corridor that I'm not looking where I'm going, and crash into one of the good old boys who backs away into the wall. At the same time, he drops a stack of paperwork onto the floor.

It's Raggi. The fat boy in black.

'What on earth's going on?' he gasps.

I put the briefcase aside, pick up papers from the floor and hand them to him.

'Why are most of your colleagues massive chauvinists and arrogant wankers?' I spit out.

He grins back.

'Who've you been talking to now?'

'Haraldur.'

'Our very own knight in shining armour.'

'Rusty armour, more like.'

'Hey, Stella. Calm yourself down.'

Raggi invites me into his office.

The old guy fills every inch of the high-backed office chair. He's been battling for years against his body's fat genes, and losing.

His bald patch has also spread over the last few years. It's like the expanding desert in Africa. To this old pal's great distress. He's taken desperate measures. It's all been shaved off.

I can't take my eyes off his naked, shiny scalp.

'When did retreat become the best form of attack?' I ask.

'When something is inevitable, the idea is to make it look as if you have a choice in the matter,' Raggi says, making himself comfortable in the chair. 'It's called strategic management.'

'Ha, ha.'

He's still smoking, even though the heart specialist told him to pack it in after the operation. That was when a whole string of the old guy's arteries were replaced.

I sit down. Try to relax. Look out of the window at Hlemmur where the buses are coming and going. And where the down-and-outs hustle for the price of a bottle of forgetfulness.

There's a large picture on the wall behind Raggi's desk. It's a village somewhere along the coast. A row of houses cluster at the edge of a broad fjord, beneath a sheer mountainside.

'Where's that?'

'That's where I started my police career,' he smiles. 'Sometimes I feel I shouldn't ever have left Bíldudalur.'

Bíldudalur?

The old newspaper clippings that Hákon Hákonarson carefully kept for decades on end flash through my mind. That's the article about the fire at Jórunnarstaðir. It quoted a policeman in Bíldudalur called Ragnar Jónsson.

Fat Raggi?

12

Fat Raggi forty-two years ago?

I try to imagine what this good lad could have looked like back in 1972. Thick hair? Slim? Rippling muscles beneath his black uniform?

Unless he's always been fat?

'What's it like being the king of a small town?' I ask.

Raggi leans back in his chair. His belly lifts into my line of sight.

'Back then nobody in Bíldudalur looked on a policeman as anything special. They'd try and play practical jokes on us, especially at weekends,' he says. 'There were just the two of us in the force there. Me and Halldór. And he was getting close to retirement and took things easy.'

'So you got to do the lousy jobs?'

'Halldór left dealing with the pissheads and the country dances to me, and the tourists who got stranded,' he says. 'Otherwise it was a very relaxed job and an absolute paradise compared to what was waiting for me when I came to Reykjavík.'

'What brought you down south?'

'Personal reasons.'

'When was that?'

'I moved south in the autumn of 1981, and I've been here next door to Hlemmur ever since,' he said with a smirk.

'Do you recall the twins at Jórunnarstaðir?'

There's a serious look on his face.

'You mean Ási and Röggi?'

'I guess so. Their names were Ásvaldur and Rögnvaldur.'

He leans forward over the desk.

'What about them?'

'Someone told me about them the other day.'

'Who remembers them?'

'Hákon Hákonarson.'

His eyes narrow.

'Hákon?' he asks thoughtfully. 'Hákon from Hvítanes?'

'He died a few days ago.'

'That's right. I saw the death notice in the paper.'

'Did you know the old man?'

'I used to meet Hákon and his brother Jörundur now and again when they came to Bíldudalur to buy provisions or have a good time,' Raggi replies. 'Hvítanes was one of the most isolated farms in Arnarfjörður. It's a place that was often cut off in the winter, and could only be reached on skis or a snowmobile. It wasn't much better in the summer, with a road that was either flooded or blocked by falling boulders. As far as I recall, Jörundur went down south to study, and then went to Copenhagen, while Hákon took over the farm, growing a few crops and breaking in horses.'

'Did you see what was left of Jórunnarstaðir after the fire?'

He shifts in his chair.

'Yes. It was a terrible sight,' he says, his voice heavy. 'That was the first time I saw bodies that were in such a bad way. That's not something you forget.'

'Hákon didn't have much love for them.'

'The twins were certainly a handful of trouble, even though they came from a good home and their father had been the bank manager,' Raggi says. 'They got involved with drugs in Copenhagen and were still at it when they came back home. I remember not long after the twins came back home and moved into Jórunnarstaðir we had a tip-off that they were selling youngsters dope and moonshine. Halldór and I called on them a few times, but we were never able to pin anything on them.'

'So you must have seen Hjördís? And Ásthildur?'

Raggi's brows knit. It doesn't look like the names ring any bells.

'Ásvaldur was married to Hjördís Eyjólfsdóttir,' I add by way of explanation. 'Ásthildur was their baby daughter.'

My good lad shakes his head.

'I don't remember them,' he says. 'It's a long time ago. A good forty years.'

'So you don't know what became of Ásthildur?'

'No.'

Raggi sends me a sharp glance. There's an inquisitive look in his eyes.

'What's your interest in this family?'

'Hákon asked me to trace Ásthildur.'

'What for?'

'It's not as if it's a secret,' I reply. 'Hákon was adamant up to the day he died that he was the child's father, and not Ásvaldur.'

'Is that so?'

'That's all I know.'

He looks up at the ceiling.

'Y'know, I'm not sure I didn't hear mentioned a girl and a baby having been at Jórunnarstaðir, but I never saw them.'

'Hjördís died that same year, 1972, and the baby was adopted.'

'I don't remember that. Adoptions weren't something that concerned the police.'

'Was there any suspicion of arson?'

Raggi jerks upright in his chair.

'Where? At Jórunnarstaðir?'

'Yes.'

'No, that was never considered. Why d'you ask?'

'Pure curiosity.'

I smile, and get to my feet.

Fat Raggi doesn't believe me. He's a whole lot smarter than you'd think from looking at him.

His inquisitive gaze follows me out of the door.

13

Tuesday 6th January

Reykjavík's finest have made no progress on the murder at Bessastaðir.

They reply to reporters' questions with platitudes, stating that the investigation is at an early stage. Even though a bunch of people had been questioned, so far there's no suspect.

Playing it this close to the chest means that the internet rumour mill is running at full tilt, and online it's mostly impossible to figure out what's true and what's lies.

There are anonymous claims online that Benedikt must have been murdered by someone who had been with him at the President's reception that Friday. The conclusion is that the guilty party has to be among society's most powerful individuals. Others argue that this murder is the man on the street fighting back, that this is a foretaste of what other wealthy banksters can expect if the courts don't get round to locking them up.

What didn't help stem the flood of anonymous online blather was that the boys in black hadn't even confirmed exactly when this wealthy man had lost his life. Had guests from Iceland and abroad sipped wine with the President at his residence that Friday afternoon? Or had it been that evening? Or even sometime during the night?

There's an early morning call from Máki with the latest gossip.

'Do you know anything about the candlesticks?' he asks with incredulity in his voice.

'I don't know anything.'

'There's a rumour going around that someone nicked the candlesticks from the church,' Máki says. 'Normally there are six candlesticks on the altar. Did you notice them?'

I hesitate. That's even though I recall clearly what the priest said in the church, and the absence of candlesticks on the altar.

From my point of view, I don't want to involve myself publicly in a police investigation that's none of my business.

'Call the Reverend Jóhannes,' I reply after a pause. 'He knows.'

'Aha!'

Máki ends the call quickly.

My advertisement appeared in today's papers, with a photo of Ilona.

Have you seen this woman?

There are a short, sharp couple of lines beneath the picture.

Sigvaldi Auðólfsson, owner of the El Dorado night club, sent this woman to a private party on 27ᵗʰ December. She has not been seen since. Anyone who can provide information concerning Ilona's movements or whereabouts is requested to contact Stella Blómkvist Legal Services.

'Any responses?' I ask Lísa Björk.

'Sigvaldi's called a few times,' she says with a mischievous smirk.

Porno Valdi is pretty livid, when I finally answer.

He complains that he's had to spend all morning fending off questions from the media about Ilona's whereabouts.

'I have instructed my lawyers to demand that you publicly apologise for this stunt,' he says, his voice heavy with menace. 'Otherwise you'll be sued for libel and causing reputational damage.'

'That's odd,' I snap back. 'I didn't imagine that a porn peddler like you would have a reputation to worry about.'

'Nobody messes with Sigvaldi Auðólfsson and comes out on top. You ought to know that better than anyone.'

'If you're in touch with Ilona, then get her to call me or Dagnija, and it's case over,' I say. 'If not, then leave me alone. Threats don't work on me. You might as well just go out to Grótta and piss into the wind.'

One of the state TV newshounds calls me in the afternoon. He wants a comment on Sigvaldi Auðólfsson's assertion that Ilona had texted him to confirm that she would return to work in mid-January.

'Nothing has been heard from Ilona since the 27th,' I reply. 'Her friends are concerned that she may have come to harm, and she is in the habit of being in touch every day. That's the reason for advertising for information about her movements. We want to know where Ilona is. And whether she's alive or dead.'

'You suspect that she may be dead?' the newshound demands, immediately excited.

'She's clearly still here in Iceland, as Sigvaldi Auðólfsson has her passport. But I know nothing about her whereabouts or her wellbeing. As you can imagine, the concern for her becomes stronger the longer she isn't in contact with those closest to her. The same applies to our suspicions relating to those who refuse to provide any assistance in locating Ilona.'

Take that, Porno Valdi!

It's close to midnight and I'm under the bedclothes. I'm about to nod off when the mobile buzzing brings me back to wakefulness.

It takes a moment to work out who is on the phone,

chattering in bad English. Dagnija's voice is so low. It's like she's frightened, or in hiding.

'Where are you?' I ask.

'Copenhagen,' Dagnija replies. 'Has Ilona been found?'

'Why did you leave the country so suddenly?'

'Sigvaldi made me. He drove me straight to the airport and took my phone.'

'Do you have your passport?'

'No, she took it at Kastrup.'

'Who?'

'The woman who runs New Baltic.'

'Is she in Copenhagen?'

'Yes, and she threatens me all the time.'

'What kind of threats?'

'She's told me not to speak to anyone in Iceland. She said I'd be sent back to Latvia if I don't do exactly as I'm told.'

'Why's she making these threats?'

'I don't know. I really don't want to go back home. There's no future there.'

There's anguish in Dagnija's voice.

'Sigvaldi says that Ilona sent him a text on New Year's Day.'

'I don't believe it.'

'Why?'

'If Ilona had got to her phone to send Sigvaldi a message, then she would have been in touch with me as well. I'm sure of it.'

'Sigvaldi's behaviour has been appalling,' I say. 'He has something to hide. No two ways about it.'

'I can feel that something bad has happened to Ilona,' Dagnija says.

'I put an advert in the papers this morning, asking for information about her.'

'Good.'

'I'm hoping someone gets in touch. Somebody must have seen her.'

Dagnija sighs.

'I have to go,' she whispers.

'Can I reach you on this number?'

'No. No, I need to return the phone before the guy wonders where it is.'

'You stole a phone?'

'No, just borrowed it. I don't have money to buy a phone.'

'How can I contact you?'

'You can't. I have to take care. I'll try and call again.'

Dagnija ends the call without another word.

Now I'm too angry to get back to sleep.

Porno Valdi and this New Baltic company treat Dagnija like a prisoner. Or a concubine. It's as if they own every bit of her.

Maybe that's exactly the way it is. It's a colossal lie that slavery in Europe no longer exists.

Porno Valdi's over-the-top responses are making me nervous. This just confirms my suspicion that Dagnija's right. Something terrible has happened to her friend.

14

Wednesday 7th January

I'm behind the wheel of my silver steed. It's early in the morning. I'm heading for Hlemmur.

The city's finest are questioning Robertas again.

Gunnbjörn, Bolli, Robertas and Svanhvít are all waiting for me in the little room where the interview is taking place. The air in there is thick and heavy.

The barrel-chested drug squad supremo plays it as if he has a handful of trumps. He reckons he has new information from overseas. That's info from his opposite numbers in Kaunas and from the European plods, Europol.

'You've quite a colourful career behind you, my boy,' he says, thoughtfully inspecting Robertas.

My client shrugs once Svanhvít has translated that into Lithuanian.

'The police have repeatedly arrested you for fighting, assault and all kinds of narcotics offences.'

'Those were all youthful mistakes,' Svanhvít translates. 'He says he has never been in prison.'

'No. And I find that absolutely remarkable,' the chief replies. 'You seem to have evaded justice, and at most been sentenced to a few fines. That tells me someone's protecting you.'

An arrogant smirk flashes across Robertas's face.

'Indeed, God is on my side,' he replies.

Gunnbjörn peers at a photocopy of a map on the desk in front of him. It shows Northern Europe in black and white. A broad line has been drawn on it, in red.

As far as I can see the line runs from Lithuania and southwards through Germany to Holland, and from there back north through Jutland. It goes all the way to *Norræna's* port of call.

'Why didn't you take the shortest route from Kaunas to Denmark?' Gunnbjörn asks, watching Robertas closely.

'That's what I did.'

'Nope. With the assistance of our colleagues overseas, we've traced the route this BMW took from Lithuania to Iceland and we can prove that you didn't take the direct route,' Gunnbjörn replies. 'We know that instead of taking the route that would pass through the north of Germany and into Jutland, you took a long detour and went via Amsterdam. Why?'

'Robertas states that this is a misunderstanding and that he did not travel to Holland on the way,' Svanhvít says.

'We know he went to Amsterdam,' the drug squad chief repeats. 'What was he doing in Holland?'

But Robertas digs in his heels.

'What information do you have to back up this allegation?' I ask.

'Solid evidence.'

'Let's see it.'

'This is information that's not for distribution at this moment.'

'Unless it's fiction? Leading my client into a trap?'

'That doesn't even merit a response.'

Gunnbjörn leans over the table. He stares unrelentingly at Robertas. He doesn't let up in demanding explanations for his trip to Amsterdam. He suggests that he went there to fetch the narcotics that were hidden in the car's fuel tank.

But my client doesn't give way. He's adamant that all he

did was to deliver the car to Iceland, that he's never been to Holland.

Robertas repeats that he had no idea that the car was to be used to smuggle drugs to Iceland. He says he's the innocent victim of ruthless men he doesn't know personally. He doesn't even know their real names.

The chief will have to settle for this conclusion – for the moment.

'This stubborn attitude is going to hurt your client badly,' he says, getting to his feet. 'If Robertas refuses to co-operate, then his sentence is simply going to be heavier than it would otherwise be.'

'I have yet to see any evidence that he knew there were narcotics in the vehicle,' I reply firmly. It's as if I believe it myself.

Gunnbjörn gathers his paperwork and heads for the door.

'Everyone who travels around Europe by car leaves a trail behind them that's fairly easy to trace,' he says. 'The Dutch police are on the trail already and it's a question of how long it takes before they collar his pals in Amsterdam, and then Robertas will be in deep shit.'

Once the cops are gone, I go over the situation with my client. I tell him the truth. The outlook's bleak.

'First and foremost, you need to think of your own interests,' I conclude. 'How long are you prepared to spend in prison in Iceland? Two to three years? Or five to six?'

Svanhvít translates.

Robertas replies that he understands the situation. But he doesn't have a choice. So he's not going to change his story.

'Tell him that if they can prove that he's lying about the trip to Amsterdam, then there's no doubt the judge will give him an extra year or two.'

They discuss in Lithuanian for some time.

Svanhvít is clearly making an effort to explain things for

Robertas, who doesn't seem satisfied with the answers. His raises his voice. He rounds on her, and sounds angry.

'What's he asking?'

Svanhvít sighs.

'He, well, he says he doesn't understand all this about Amsterdam,' she replies. 'He's adamant that he's never been there. If that's the case, then the police must be confusing two cars.'

I take a long look at the court interpreter.

The conversation with Robertas seems to have left her nerves jangling. A flush has crept into her plump cheeks. She repeatedly wets her lips with the tip of her tongue.

'I just want him to fully appreciate the seriousness of his situation,' I say. 'Nobody can help him if he can't help himself.'

As soon as Svanhvít has translated, he goes back to deluging her with questions. He takes no notice of me.

'All right,' I say and finally get to my feet. 'Thank you, Svanhvít. This conversation is over.'

Robertas isn't satisfied. He says something to the interpreter.

'He says he wants to continue the discussion,' Svanhvít says.

'Later,' I say, opening the door.

Bolli handcuffs Robertas and leads him from the room.

'I think it's dawning on him,' Svanhvít apologises. 'That's why he was so animated just now.'

'Better late than never.'

I leave her in the corridor. I hurry out of the blackbirds' headquarters, and march over to my car.

It's getting cool. It looks like there'll be an overnight frost. That'll mean black ice on the city streets.

I sit behind my silver steed's wheel, but don't start the engine right away.

Why am I feeling a faint unease deep inside, before heading out into the cool breeze blowing through Hlemmur?

It's because something isn't right. Things aren't the way they should be.

That's the only possible explanation.

Or what?

Feminine intuition is the smoke alarm of the soul, as Mother said.

15

Thursday 8th January

She called ahead. I mean the red-haired girl with the green eyes.

Rósalind was hesitant on the phone when she called just after midnight. She came across as consumed by doubt over whether she was doing the right thing by coming to me.

'I absolutely don't want to meet at your office,' she said.

'Why not?'

'It's best if we aren't seen together.'

'Is speaking to me seen as a serious transgression within the Reykjavík force?'

'You'll understand when you know what's going on.'

'I take my daughter to nursery at eight,' I said. 'Meet me somewhere on the way.'

That morning I set off on foot for the nursery.

Sóley Árdís is half-asleep in the pushchair when Rósalind makes her unexpected appearance at my side. She's jogging, wearing a black track suit and white trainers.

Her long red hair's tied in a ponytail.

She's been sweating with the exertion. But she's not even slightly out of breath.

'We're talking a hundred per cent confidentially, aren't we?'

'Of course.'

'I was knocked off balance when I saw the picture in the paper.'

'What picture?'

'The one in the advertisement for the girl from Latvia.'

I stop in my tracks. Rósalind glances around as if making sure nobody's watching us as I stare at her.

'You I knew Ilona?' I demand.

'No. Not like that. I just saw her that one time.'

'Where?'

'You said in the ad that she had gone to a party on the 27th and hadn't been seen since.'

'Yes. And?'

'We had a party at the police college that night.'

'And?'

'The guys brought this girl along around midnight.'

I catch hold of Rósalind's shoulder, pulling her around to face me. I stare into her green eyes.

'You're telling me that Ilona was the entertainment for you lot at the police college the night she disappeared?'

'Yes.'

'Do you know when she left?'

'No. I know it must have been before one.'

'How so?'

'I had to go outside for half an hour. When I came back at around one o'clock, she was gone.'

'Who with?'

'The boys, I guess.'

'Which boys?'

'Glúmur and Eiríkur. They brought her to the party.'

I immediately recall the names of the two blackbirds who had been with Rósalind that night we met downtown. That was the celibate New Year's Eve.

'Ilona told her friend that she was going to a party in a cool jeep.'

'Glúmur has a flashy Land Cruiser.'

'Have you asked the boys where Ilona went after the party was over?'

'Yes. I recognised the girl the moment I saw the paper and mentioned it to Glúmur when I saw him yesterday.'

'And?'

'He was just angry. Said it definitely wasn't the same girl.'

'Really?'

'I thought it was weird, because I was quite certain. So I offered to show him the pictures I took on my phone.'

'What pictures?'

'I took a few pictures when the girl started to strip for the boys and sent them to my friend.'

'And this wasn't enough to convince Glúmur?'

'No. He's adamant that these are two different girls.'

Rósalind fell silent.

'Glúmur told me to delete the photos from my phone,' she added.

'Why?'

'He said we couldn't let it get out that they had brought a stripper into the police college. It's a serious contravention of the rules, there would be hell to pay and we'd be thrown out of the force.'

'So you didn't delete the pictures?'

Rósalind shakes her head.

'That's great. Let's see them.'

She hesitates.

'I can't,' she says at last.

'Why not?'

'I lost my phone on that same shift.'

'Lost it?'

'Yes, I suppose so. Anyway, it's nowhere to be found.'

Rósalind's account gets stranger by the minute.

'You mean your phone was stolen?' I suggest.

'At first I thought I'd just lost the phone, but yesterday Stína lost her phone as well, and that's when I started to get suspicious.'

'Who's Stína?'

'I sent her the pictures from the party.'

'Aha.'

'Exactly. I didn't think it could be a coincidence.'

'Of course not.'

'When I pressed Glúmur about it during the shift last night and wanted to know if he'd taken my phone, he turned aggressive and threatening.'

'Threatening, how?'

'He said that all of our careers would be in jeopardy if the Commissioner heard about the stripper, and he said he wasn't going to let himself be thrown out of the force because I had been so stupid as to take those pictures.'

'What a wanker...'

'All the same, I kept on about it, and Glúmur told me that if I was really so stupid as to not see what's in my own interest, then he and his pals have ways to make sure I keep my mouth shut for good.'

'What did he mean by that?'

Rósalind shrugs.

'Glúmur was simply threatening something serious will happen to me if I say anything,' she says. 'He's well connected inside the force. He has highly placed relatives who can make or break careers.'

'What relatives are we talking about here?'

'His father's Aðalsteinn, who has responsibility for the police college.'

This is new information and I try to digest it.

'You're a hundred per cent certain that Ilona was with these two guys the night she disappeared?' I ask after a pause.

'Yes.'

'And now they're making threats to keep you quiet?'

'That's it.'

'Could you be mistaken?'

Rósalind shakes her head.

'But I no longer have any evidence,' she says in a dull tone. 'If I make a formal report stating that Ilona was stripping that night at the police college, they'd force me out of the police.'

'It's clear to me that you don't have any easy choices,' I reply. 'But I have to recommend that you tell your superiors the truth.'

'That's not going to be any use as long as the guys all say I'm lying.'

'Porno Valdi must be aware that Ilona went with Glúmur and Eiríkur that night. He should be able to corroborate your testimony.'

'I'd never dare to put my future in the hands of someone like him,' she says.

'And I understand that perfectly,' I reply. 'But if you're convinced that Ilona was present at the police college the night she disappeared, then you have a duty to inform your superiors. To my mind, it's that simple.'

She shuffles her feet restlessly for a while.

'I'm going to think it over,' she says at last, turns and jogs back the way she came.

The long red ponytail swings in time with every step.

16

Porno Valdi's not speaking to me.

I tried a couple of times earlier today to call him. No luck.

By six o'clock I've had enough. I call Cora, and wrap up my little bundle of joy in a red snowsuit and pink shoes. The silver steed takes me to Sissi and Cora's place out on Álftanes. I leave my baby with them for a while and head downtown. I park up behind El Dorado, next to the grey dumpster.

Almost everyone connects Sigvaldi Auðólfsson's name with the city's pornification that really got going in the last decade of the twentieth century. He grabbed the opportunity the moment the city authorities decided to license pole dancing joints. Titty bars popped up everywhere around the city. When supply had started to outstrip demand, Porno Valdi made full use of his political links to strengthen his position. Competitors closed their doors one after another, until Sigvaldi was left with the field all to himself as Iceland's undisputed porn kingpin.

There are a few guys lounging in armchairs in the main bar. The lights are dim. Others stand at the bar itself. The personal dances take place in private rooms where drunk guys can spend thousands in just one night. That's for a close-up and personal lap dance. Plus there's cheap champagne at crazy prices.

What the hell for? These pathetic guys don't even get an orgasm out of it.

Sheesh!

Porno Valdi's office is on the next floor up.

There's a pair of hefty bouncers at the bottom of the stairs. I recognise one of them. This is the crop-headed thug I sent last time to tell Sigvaldi to come and talk to me.

He takes my card. He glances at the well-chosen words I've scrawled on the back. It's something short and sharp that nobody else understands. He sets off up the stairs, lumbering his way upwards.

My message has the desired effect. It was to the point: *Are you going to talk to me now? Or after I've made mincemeat of you in the press?*

Porno Valdi's gone downhill since I saw him last, and that was a few years back.

His cheeks have filled out with flab. There's a spare tyre round his middle. He's given up bothering about any kind of exercise, that's clear enough.

But there's no let-up in his vanity. Last time I saw him he was greying at the temples. Now his hair gleams black. Clearly dyed.

Porno Valdi's office resembles a posh parlour. There's a leather sofa on the right, behind a low coffee table topped with a thick slab of pale marble. On the left is a massive flatscreen and closed cabinets made of expensive wood.

Jónsteinn Ingólfsson has made himself comfortable on the sofa with his knees spread wide and his bald head shining. He's a ginger kind of guy, of around forty. His job title is El Dorado's entertainments manager. In reality he's the porn king's gofer and fixer.

Sigvaldi sits up straight in a chair that looks more like a throne, on the far side of a vast brown desk.

'What d'you want?' he snarls.

I sit myself down on the cold marble, next to the entertainments manager. Legs crossed, I stare into the porn king's eyes.

'I want you to call your pal and tell him to have Ilona call me.'

The two of them quickly exchange glances.

'What friend are you talking about?' Sigvaldi asks.

'I know where you sent Ilona that night,' I snap back. 'And who picked her up from your place.'

'How do you know?'

'That's irrelevant. I have solid testimony that Ilona was stripping at the police college the same night she disappeared. Don't bother to deny it.'

Jónsteinn and Sigvaldi glance at each other.

'I know that Glúmur Aðalsteinsson picked her up in his Land Cruiser at around eleven,' I continue.

'So what?' Porno Valdi asks.

'Their party was over at one,' Jónsteinn says in his reedy voice. 'After that the girl went off somewhere by herself.'

'Glúmur was going to send her back here in a taxi,' Sigvaldi adds. 'She turned that down and said that she had been offered a lift.'

'That's what he said?'

'Yes.'

'Who was supposed to have offered her a lift from the police college?'

'She didn't say anything about that to Glúmur.'

'He reckons he didn't see who collected Ilona?'

'No. Glúmur went home as soon as her turn was over, before she left.'

'Alone?'

'No. Eiríkur went with him.'

'Do you genuinely imagine I believe this fucking bullshit?'

'Glúmur has never lied to me,' Sigvaldi says. 'His story tallies with Eiríkur's.'

'So that means you have no idea where Ilona is?'

'The girl sent a text on New Year's Day, saying she'd be back at work in the middle of January,' he growls. 'I'm happy to believe that.'

'I don't believe you or Glúmur.'

Sigvaldi shrugs.

'Why did you punish Dagnija?' I ask. 'You threw her out of the country as if she's some worthless slave. Because she came to me?'

He leans sharply forward.

'I was instructed to send her to Copenhagen on the first available flight,' he retorts. 'The agency thought it was bad enough Ilona being in hiding, without Dagnija wreaking havoc for no reason.'

'Dagnija has no passport and no money. She's like a prisoner there.'

'I know nothing about that.'

'So who does?'

Sigvaldi grins evilly.

'Maybe you should ask your friend,' he says.

I don't like the malevolent look in his eye.

'Meaning what?'

'Are you trying to tell me you don't know who runs New Baltic Models International?'

'Should I?'

'Of course.'

'Why?'

'Because your friend runs the company.'

'What fucking friend?' I snap.

'Ludmilla,' Porno Valdi replies with a grin.

I feel suddenly sick. But I tough it out. Try to let no feelings show.

'New Baltic has achieved a leading position on the Nordic market over the last few years under her management,' Sigvaldi continues. 'Her girls are the preferred ones at most of the big strip clubs in Scandinavia and here. This last year all my girls have come through New Baltic.'

'You're telling me that Ludmilla told you to put Dagnija on the next flight to Copenhagen?'

'That's it.'

'She told you herself?'

'Yes. She called me and demanded I send the girl the same day. I did what she asked for, because Dagnija and Ilona are her babes.'

Jónsteinn laughs from the sofa, joyfully. He's like an evil street kid taking delight in tearing the wings off a beautiful butterfly.

17

Friday 9th January

Sóley Árdís has eyes that are bright and blue.

They're her dad's eyes.

The Reverend Finnbogi hasn't the faintest idea that he has a child. It's none of his business. For the moment, at any rate.

Maybe at some point, in a few years. That'll be when Sóley Árdís starts to ask why she doesn't have a dad like the other kids do.

Until then, she's all mine.

The worst of it is that I wasn't that lucky, to be fatherless when I was small.

But that's all in the past. I was finally able to bury all the misery of my early years along with Karl Blómkvist at his funeral in the old home town in the east. And I managed to spark a new life at the same time, right there under the altarpiece of the old wooden church.

I choose to see my daughter as having been the work of just one parent, more or less.

The city's finest are pushing hard for Robertas to finger the Icelandic buyers of the amphetamines that were hidden in those sealed containers in the fuel tank of the BMW he brought to Iceland.

Fat Raggi calls me at dinner time.

'We have reason to believe that Robertas knows more than we had initially suspected about the crimes behind this than the standard mules we've been picking up recently,' he says.

'What makes you think that?'

'We've been informed that when he came here last October, Robertas didn't smuggle any dope, but he brought some important information from the top dogs in Lithuania for the people at the Icelandic end of the operation.'

'What evidence do you have for this?'

'That's confidential.'

'I have to assume that you have an informer at the centre of this operation,' I continue. 'Is this person here or overseas?'

Raggi hesitates.

'You're asking a favour, right?'

'Our source is here in Iceland,' he replies cautiously. 'He has indicated that Robertas is no normal mule.'

'From the word go he didn't strike me as someone likely to spill the beans.'

'You could have some influence on him.'

'Only if the outcome is a more lenient sentence.'

'You know that the police can't make promises of that nature. Sentencing is entirely at the discretion of the courts.'

'Raggi, I know exactly how the system works,' I retort. 'You can influence the judge's decision behind the scenes.'

'Check it out,' he says. 'That's all I'm asking.'

The plods are getting desperate if they're getting Raggi to call me.

There's no ruling out that my client knows more than he's letting on. That's especially if Sergei was the one who sent Robertas to Iceland with the goods. That's because Sergei is certainly far from being some low-grade hoodlum in the Baltic underworld.

Robertas could have some valuable information. He could have names that could be bargaining chips for a shorter sentence. And prison is inevitable, regardless of how loud he sings for the cops.

I still enjoy treating myself on a Friday night. I go out less than I used to. A bar crawl every other weekend's enough these days. It's even down to once a month sometimes. That's when hunger forces me out into the night.

Age is playing its part, and the responsibilities of parenthood.

On this evening's menu is bouillabaisse, French fish soup. It's a recipe from Alice B. Toklas and Gertrude Stein when they first went to Marseilles. Except that I have to make do with four varieties of fish instead of seven – a little monkfish, a fillet of plaice, tiny shrimps, a chunk of Westfjords catfish. I top it up with a decent wine. French, of course. *Chablis Grand Cru Blanchots.*

Mmmm!

Sóley Árdís sits opposite me at the dining table in the living room. She's in her highchair, full and happy. She's a smiling ray of sunshine who lights up the cold everyday gloom.

Sometimes it's so good to not be alone.

I fell for Ludmilla the very first moment I saw her. That was even though the circumstances were as bad as they could be, the assault on her younger sister who now rests in Icelandic soil.

Right away I wanted to lose myself in the depths of those wide, dark eyes, and to press greedy kisses to her deep red lips, bury my face in her long black hair.

She was the big love of my life. She still has a direct line to my heart. That's also because we so rarely have time to enjoy being together.

My life is here. Hers is in Latvia.

It goes without saying that I knew from the outset about

her links to Porno Valdi. She'd been one of his strippers when we first met. She seemed to not only know the business inside out, she also had some murky connections to the underworld in the Baltic States, where her father was some kind of Godfather figure.

I never wanted to know more. I convinced myself that Ludmilla's business in foreign countries was no concern of mine. I always avoided asking any questions.

But now there's no getting around it.

When Sóley Árdís is asleep, I sit at the computer and compose a message to send to Ludmilla's email address in Lithuania. I set out briefly my dealings with Dagnija, the fruitless search for Ilona, and the vile conversation with Porno Valdi. I'm looking for clear, unambiguous answers.

18

Saturday 10th January

The District Commissioner's not amused. Apparatchiks tend to lose it whenever they have to step even a little outside their comfortable daily routines.

'There'll be an announcement next week, requesting applications to the estate,' was what the Commissioner's deputy had said last week. 'On the other hand, we have no information relating to this alleged daughter...'

'You have Hákon's written statement and wishes,' I interrupted.

'According to the documents we have, the courts have already refused to lift the legally required confidentiality concerning the adoption of the child,' he replied. 'Seeking a change to that decision isn't something that comes within our purview.'

'Which means what?'

'It means we have no legal grounds to consider that Ásthildur Ásvaldsdóttir may have been the daughter of Hákon Hákonarson,' the deputy said. 'That's aside from the obvious fact that this Ásthildur no longer exists, in legal terms.'

I growled my disgruntlement. I told him to look into the confidential paperwork stored away in the system relating to Ásthildur's adoption in 1972. Then he could look at comparing her genetics to Hákon's.

'This woman has a right to know her true paternity,' I told him. 'And she also has a right to inherit her father's estate.'

But the deputy wouldn't be moved.

'We won't be making any enquiries into this,' he insisted. And that means he's put the ball in my court.

That's why right now I'm heading down to Kópavogur. This is where the brother of the deceased lives, Jörundur Hákonarson the engineer, in the new extension to the Sunnuhlíð nursing home.

He's in a wheelchair, bald and beardless, his cheeks sunken.

'Come in,' he says, reversing the wheelchair into the room. 'Would you like to sit on the sofa?'

His arms tremble. They don't stop when he grasps his right hand with the left.

'Parkinson's?'

'Yes. Unfortunately, the illness gets steadily worse,' he says.

The room is like a mini version of Jörundur's home. The walls are packed with photographs, family pictures. There are a couple of paintings as well.

I sit in the leather chair, a Chesterfield.

Jörundur doesn't have the use of his legs, thanks to a car crash on Hellisheiði.

'He and his wife were on their way to Hveragerði when a drunk driver swerved across the road, not far from the truck stop up there,' Lísa Björk reported after having checked the man's background for me. 'His wife died, and so did the drunk, but the doctors managed to save Jörundur's life. From what I've been told, he would have preferred to have died as well.'

'Hákon told me about his will sometime before he died,' Jörundur says.

'What do you think?' I ask. 'Was there something in this with Ásthildur, or is this just wishful thinking?'

'Hjördís stayed with him at Hvítanes for a couple of months in the summer of 1970, that's for sure,' Jörundur replies. 'But at the time I was studying in Copenhagen, so I wasn't a witness to what did – or didn't – go on between them.'

'Were they alone at the farm?'

'No, Eygló Arnardóttir was there as well. She was our father's housekeeper every summer, and she kept that up for a few years after he passed away.'

'Is she still alive?'

'The last I heard, she was still alive and well in Bíldudalur.'

'Did you ask her about Hákon and Hjördís?'

Jörundur shook his head.

'In fact, it's because of me that Hjördís spent that summer with my brother.'

'How so?'

'Look, I knew Hjördís and also her parents. They lived for a while at Jórunnarstaðir near Bíldudalur, but moved south to Reykjavík when she was in her early teens,' Jörundur says. 'Hjördís was always painting as a youngster and she spent some time studying art, and then went to continue her studies in Copenhagen, and by then I had already been there for a couple of years. We'd often meet at Jónshús and occasionally at my place during those first few months she was there, and then we lost touch.'

'What happened?'

'I heard that she had settled in Christiania, and this was just at the time when going to the bad was the pinnacle of freedom. It was none of my business, but then her parents in Reykjavík got in touch with me and asked me to check on her, as they had heard all kinds of stories of their daughter's lifestyle. I found that Hjördís was living in a commune with two other Icelanders, Ásvaldur and Rögnvaldur, plus a bunch of other junkies of different nationalities. I stopped by one evening and met Hjördís.'

She was clearly deep in Morpheus's grip. It was genuinely awful to see her, but she said she didn't need any help from me or anyone else.'

'I see.'

'Her parents were naturally deeply upset when they heard the news,' Jörundur continues. 'Her father travelled to Copenhagen and I went with him to speak to Hjördís. That was when it turned out that she was married to Ásvaldur, who said he was perfectly capable of looking after his wife without any interference from parents.'

Jörundur reaches for a small carton on the table, puts the straw in his mouth with fingers that shake, and drinks.

'In the spring of 1970 Hjördís was taken to hospital in Copenhagen, more dead than alive,' he says after a long pause. 'She'd overdosed on heroin. Her parents came to Copenhagen and were at their daughter's side in the hospital, and finally got her to agree to treatment. But Hjördís flatly refused to enter any kind of institution, so some other solution was required, and finally Hvítanes occurred to me as it's so remote and nobody ever goes near the place.'

He glances at one of the pictures on the wall. It's a painting of a farm on a green hill not far from a rocky shore. The farmhouse itself, at the centre of the picture, is pale blue.

'The blue house by the shore is Hvítanes,' he says.

'An unusual colour for a farmhouse,' I say.

'True. But the painter was someone out of the ordinary,' Jörundur replies with a faint smile. 'Hjördís painted the house this colour during the summer of 1970, and later on she painted this picture.'

I know nothing about art. It's not my department. But there's something about the painting. Something intangible that gives it an added depth.

It's as if Jörundur's reading my mind.

'There's a particular joy to this picture,' he says. 'I think

85

it's the joy of life itself, the joy of existence.'

'But that was short-lived joy?'

'Sadly, yes. Hjördís returned to Copenhagen in the autumn, the child was born in the spring of 1972 and for a while she seemed to be doing well. But by the time they came to live at Jórunnarstaðir that autumn, Hjördís was a user again, as those twins were always deep in drugs.'

'But she escaped the fire?'

'Yes. Hjördís was being treated in hospital in Reykjavík when Jórunnarstaðir caught fire. But she was still hooked, and that's why they took the child from her.'

'Who did?'

'The Child Welfare Committee. I think that was what tipped her over the edge.'

'In what way?'

'In that her life ended early in the winter.'

'How?'

'It's believed that she swam out to sea off Seltjarnarnes,' Jörundur replies. 'In any case, that's where her body washed ashore.'

'Did Hjördís commit suicide?'

'That was seen as the most likely explanation.'

'So why was Ásthildur adopted, rather than being taken in by her grandparents?'

'I believe that Hjördís's parents had simply given up,' Jörundur replies. 'At any rate, they didn't feel they were able to look after the child. If I recall correctly, it was Ásvaldur's father who dealt with the adoption procedure. But I was still living in Copenhagen at that time and didn't have much involvement in what was going on back home.'

'Where was Hákon while all this was happening?'

'He was tied to the farm at Hvítanes.'

'When did he first mention to you that he was Ásthildur's father?'

'That was some time after he first contacted the ministry, trying to find out what had become of the child,'

Jörundur replies. 'I reckon it must be fifteen, twenty years ago.'

'Did you believe him?'

'I knew that it could have happened, but that was all,' Jörundur says. 'Hákon was very certain, but he never told me anything about his relationship with Hjördís. He was a very private individual in that respect.'

'Which doesn't help in the slightest,' I say, getting quickly to my feet.

'What are you going to do?'

'Try to find this Ásthildur. That's the only option.'

'My brother had no success.'

'I imagine that the adoption paperwork must have been gathering dust in some office droid's filing cabinet for the last forty years. It has to be possible to track it down.'

'If the paperwork exists.'

I give Jörundur an inquiring glance.

'Meaning what?'

'Public affairs were very sloppily managed at that time,' he replies. 'Especially when influential men were concerned, such as the father of the twins at Jórunnarstaðir.'

'Was he in politics?'

'Hermann Rögnvaldsson was a bank manager and a close colleague of two of Iceland's Prime Ministers in the seventies and eighties. He was in a position to make things turn out the way he wanted.'

Hell!

But giving up isn't an option. Not now that the first blows have been struck.

'I'll do my best to break through the system and we'll see what happens,' I say in farewell, shutting the door behind me.

19

Sunday 10th January

A nightmare wakes me up.

A dream of Benedikt Björgúlfsson's bloody and broken face yet again. That's despite trying time and again to wipe from my mind that terrible sight that greeted me inside the altar rail a week ago.

The city's finest's investigation into the financier's murder still seems to be at an early stage. At least, they don't have much to say about any progress, despite the press hounding them with frequent requests for information. That tells me they haven't got far.

All the same, the papers and the TV are doing their best to keep the story alive.

The whole weekend's news revolved around the mysterious 'candlestickgate'. That's how Máki described it when he broke the story on the *News Blog*.

The police are cautious with information, but confirmed that six candlesticks are missing from the church at Bessastaðir. More than likely that happened around the same time as the murder took place. It's not as if they can keep that quiet since the Reverend Jóhannes had confirmed it in an interview with Máki.

Some of the online media flirt with digging up the history of two of these candlesticks that are associated with Niels Fuhrmann, the King of Denmark's governor of

Iceland back in the eighteenth century. These were a gift from the Danish housekeeper at Bessastaðir who was reputed to have poisoned Appolonia Schwartzkopf, the governor's betrothed, in order to give her own daughter a chance of slipping into the governor's marital bed.

'The spirit of Appolonia still lurks at Bessastaðir, seeking retribution,' as one of the bloggers put it.

The old newshound calls me at lunchtime. He seems to think I have some kind of inside information, just because I stumbled across the body.

'It's no business of mine,' I tell him, irritated.

'Hey, don't be like that, Stella,' Máki replies. 'You found Bensi's body, so it's your business all the way to the end, whether you like it or not.'

Hell...

'Quite apart from that, I'm in a spot of trouble,' he added.

'Go on.'

'I've been given an anonymous tip-off that's so off the wall that I'm wondering if it's a prank.'

I'm instantly curious.

'Let's hear it.'

'Everyone knows that the day before you found the body there was a Presidential reception for more than a hundred people, including all the top dogs in politics, business and culture. That was Bensi's last reception at Bessastaðir and the police had their usual presence, as they always do at these things.'

'Old news.'

But Máki doesn't let my negative comment hold him up.

'The authority installed a network of security cameras at Bessastaðir a few years ago, indoors and outdoors, to ensure the safety of the President and his guests.'

'That's not exactly the latest news.'

'It's been whispered to me that one of the cameras at Bessastaðir is directed at the church, so nobody can enter or leave the house of the Lord unseen.'

'Got you.'

'But you know what?'

'What?' I sigh.

'An email I received this morning states that when the investigators went to check the recordings from the Bessastaðir security cameras for that Friday, they came away empty-handed.'

'How so?'

'They found no recordings showing movement around the church that day.'

'Nothing?'

'Not a thing.'

'Says who?'

'That's the problem. It's an anonymous tip-off from an email address that I have no way of tracing back to where it came from,' Máki says. 'I've been calling around, everyone I know at the police, to get this confirmed, but nobody seems to know anything. Very mysterious.'

'Including those in charge of this investigation?'

'Yep. Them too.'

Hmmm...

'If this tip-off is correct, then there are only two possible explanations,' I say after a moment's thought. 'One is that there are no recordings. That in itself is a serious failing, but not exactly a crime. The other is that they've simply been lifted. Presumably to hide information pertaining to Benedikt's murder.'

'Exactly. It's a hell of a scandal, whichever explanation turns out to be correct,' Máki says with a triumphant flourish. 'I know for sure that access to this information is strictly limited, so if the data has been stolen, then the murderer must have been assisted by someone high up in the establishment.'

'Aha.'

'And that's why I also have to tread carefully. This

anonymous tip-off could be a poisoned chalice. I have plenty of enemies who would be delighted if I were to trip over my own feet by running a completely baseless story on the *News Blog*. I'd lose credibility.'

I find myself telling Máki to pull himself together.

'You could start cautiously, maybe by pointing out that the security system is designed to pick up any movements around Bessastaðir, including the day Benedikt was murdered. So there's no doubt that the cops must have at their disposal a list of everyone who went into the church on the day the murder was committed. That could provoke a response.'

The newshound chuckles with glee.

'That would be like sneaking a fox into the hen house! Brilliant!'

The temperature is just below zero.

I button my warm white coat up to the throat before heading out. I push the stroller easily ahead of me, past the houses of neighbours I don't know at all. I march through the cold, deserted park that's in the middle of the district, all the way to the little shopping centre where there's a bakery that's open every day of the week.

Sóley Árdís sleeps soundly while I treat myself to coffee that's thick and strong, and a delicious waffle with cream and blueberry jam.

My mobile breaks through my feeling of wellbeing.

It's Ludmilla.

Instinctively, I get a warm feeling inside that comes from simply hearing her sultry voice.

She asks how I am, and after Sóley Árdís, before I take the conversation somewhere more serious.

'You got my email?'

'I did,' she says. 'But I can't write anything. It's too dangerous.'

'What's going on?'

'I didn't know that you're helping Dagnija, and Robertas. This is a complicated affair.'

'Complicated in what way?'

Ludmilla hesitates.

'Things have been pretty strange since my father died,' she replies at last.

Her father's death is news to me.

'When did he pass away?'

'November last year. I only heard after the funeral had already taken place in Moscow.'

'I'm sorry.'

'I can't say much on the phone. That can be dangerous as well.'

'What do you mean? Is someone tapping your phone?'

'I think I need to come to Iceland so we can speak face to face.'

'Great. When?'

'In a few days. I'll let you know.'

'What about Dagnija?'

'She'll be all right. I'll check on her.'

'I want her to call me.'

Ludmilla promises to make sure Dagnija gets in touch.

'You'll have to be careful as well,' she adds. 'A lot of strange things are going on.'

My coffee's cold by the time the call is over.

Sóley Árdís stirs.

I pick her up. I let her taste the cream and the waffle as I think over Ludmilla's words of warning. This just confirms the suspicions I've had since that last conversation with Robertas.

Something's going on.

But what?

20

Monday 11ᵗʰ January

My newest client is in a bad way, both mentally and physically.

He's still in his twenties.

The city's finest seem to have made him take a shower. But there are stains on his yellow and black tee shirt and his pale jeans.

'Doesn't he have anything better to wear?' I ask Bolli. The cute young hunk shows me into the room where the statement is to be taken.

He shakes his head.

'He lives in a top-floor slum flat on Hverfisgata,' he replies. 'I gather the place is a tip.'

My client's name is Sverrir Guðbjartsson. So far that's all I know about him. Except that the boys in black are going to give him a grilling as a suspect behind a string of break-ins and thefts.

It's a long time since his matted beard was last trimmed. His mousy hair is long and unkempt.

I've seen plenty of these in my time as a lawyer, users who land in trouble. I've seen these pale, thin faces before, tired eyes and frightened glances.

Sverrir is one of these.

There's normally nothing I can do for these guys. All I can do is keep the cops from breaking them down with their aggressive, overwhelming tactics.

'Sverrir made a full and frank confession concerning these charges when the drug squad picked him up at the weekend,' Raggi says. 'That was before we felt we had good reason to have a chat with him as well.'

'Can we finish this now?' Sverrir demands.

He's itching all over, desperate for a fresh hit, and he wants to be out of here as soon as possible.

Raggi continues to list a few more break-ins. Then he glances at Sverrir.

'You're prepared to accept responsibility for all these offences, aren't you?'

'Yeah. Sure. Get it done. The whole lot.'

As soon as Sverrir has signed on the dotted line, he's on his feet.

'No, my lad,' Raggi says. 'We're not finished.'

Sverrir isn't inclined to sit back down. He finally lets himself drop into the chair. He buries his face in both hands, and groans.

The chief superintendent places the signed document to one side. He nods to Bolli.

The young stud goes out into the corridor. He's right back, this time with a long package that he places on the table in front of Raggi.

It's a long piece of metal, contained in a clear plastic bag.

I'm wondering what's going on.

The blackbirds' latest piece of evidence is a large candlestick.

'You recognise this, don't you?' Raggi asks.

Sverrir leans forward a little. He peers at the plastic bag.

'I don't remember,' he replies.

'Don't you?'

'No, don't think so. I don't remember seeing anything like that before.'

'We found this item in your room. It was under the bed where you were fast asleep when the police called to see you on Friday night.'

Sverrir snatches at a handful of his own hair.

'No, I don't remember anything like that,' he replied. 'What is it?'

'It's a candlestick,' Raggi says.

'A candlestick?' Sverrir repeats. 'I never use anything like that.'

'I suspect that you stole this candlestick.'

Sverrir shakes his head.

'In fact, I suspect that you stole more candlesticks, which we also found under your bed,' Raggi continues.

He takes photographs from a folder at his side and lays them on the table in front of us.

'Pictures of all of them,' he continues.

'Are these the candlesticks from the church at Bessastaðir?' I ask.

Raggi scowls. He doesn't answer.

'Would you be so kind as to explain how these came to be under your bed?' he asks my client.

'I don't know,' Sverrir says, rubbing his arms. 'I don't remember ever seeing anything like this at my place.'

'You must remember stealing these candlesticks. There's some weight there.'

My client again shakes his head.

Now Ragnar leans forward. He stares at Sverrir, who seems reluctant to meet his eye.

'I reckon you remember very clearly, young man.'

'No. No.'

'Oh, yes. Tell me everything, my lad, and then you can see the doctor.'

'I don't know anything about this shit.'

'We know that you stole the candlesticks when you visited your friend Sveinfríður Tómasdóttir a week ago at Bessastaðir.'

'No.'

'You remember going to see her?'

'I got a lift out to Bessastaðir to visit Sveinfríður, but I didn't steal anything.'

'She's given us a detailed statement, young man,' Raggi says, reaching for sheets of paper from the folder. 'You arrived there at around four o'clock on Friday the 2nd of January, which was nine days ago. She was still at work and suggested that you wait for her in the car she had parked outside the church. That means she allowed you to wait in her car. At around six she drove you back to the city and to your place, where you stayed together until some time during the night. Is Sveinfríður's account correct?'

Sverrir shrugs.

'I went to see her,' he replies. 'I don't remember what day it was.'

'According to her statement, you had to wait for at least an hour and a half outside the church, so you had ample time to steal these candlesticks.'

Sverrir scowls in irritation. He scratches absently at his chest.

The fat cop raises the plastic bag in both hands, holding it in front of Sverrir's face.

'We have a particular interest in this candlestick,' he says. 'I guess you know very well why.'

'*Nooo*,' he wails, instinctively backing away.

'You went into the church to steal something that you'd be able to sell for a decent amount of money,' Raggi continues. 'You liked the look of the candlesticks on the altar. But then there was a hitch, wasn't there?'

'I don't know what you're talking about.'

'Oh, yes you do, my lad. You were interrupted at the critical moment. Didn't someone come into the church?'

Sverrir shakes his head.

Raggi puts the candlestick aside and places a large photograph of Benedikt Björgúlfsson in front of us.

'This is the man who entered the church as you were stealing the candlesticks, and he ordered you to leave them alone.'

'No.'

'What did you do then? Are you going to tell us yourself?'

'Nothing. I did nothing.'

'You had this candlestick in your hand when Benedikt came into the church, didn't you?' Raggi continues, his hand grasping the evidence on the table. 'This one here.'

'No, that's not true.'

'When Benedikt told you to get out of the church right away, you hit him over the head with this candlestick, didn't you? This candlestick.'

There's horror in Sverrir's eyes as he stares at Raggi.

'No. No, I didn't hit anyone.'

'Then you wrapped the candlesticks in the altar cloth and put them in the boot of Sveinfríður's car, just as if nothing had happened, didn't you? Even though the man you had just beaten was dying of his injuries? Isn't that what happened?'

'I never went into that church,' Sverrir howls.

'You certainly did. We also found the altar cloth at your home.'

'No. No.'

He looks over at me with anguish and desperation in his eyes.

'It's not true,' he shouts out. 'I've never done anything like that. I've never hit anyone in my life.'

'Have fingerprints been identified on the candlestick?' I ask.

Raggi's focus stays on my client, without replying to me.

'On the other hand, the recordings from the security camera network at Bessastaðir will confirm whether or not Sverrir sat in the car the whole time he was waiting for this Sveinfríður,' I add. 'Shouldn't you be showing us that?'

Raggi glances sharply at me.

The sweetest smile I can manage makes his fat cheeks go pale. But he quickly regains his equilibrium.

'Sverrir Guðbjartsson,' he rasps, his eyes again on my client. 'This interview is concluded. You will be held here overnight with the status of suspect and you'll go before a judge tomorrow morning.'

'Suspected of what?' I ask.

'As things stand, he's suspected of breaking into the Bessastaðir church, theft and murder,' Raggi says, collecting the paperwork on the table. 'We'll find out tomorrow if he's still suspected of all these things.'

21

My cousin Sissi calls at the office around midday.

He's one of those lucky types who doesn't age. He still looks like a shy teenager. There's a youthful sincerity in his eyes, even though he's past thirty.

I'm planning to speak to Robertas again around two, in the state-run Litla-Hraun prison. It's full to bursting with criminals, both home-grown and foreign.

Sissi checks the equipment. There's the wireless microphone that he secreted a couple of years ago in my gilded brooch. The receiver unit is in my russet-brown briefcase. It records everything on a recorder that's no larger than a lipstick.

Svanhvít is already there. In fact, she's been there all morning translating for a number of prisoners from Lithuania. These are other mules picked up at the Leifur Eiríksson airport with dope either in their clothes or their luggage. And they spend years behind bars for this.

Robertas is still on remand. He's completely isolated. The only people he gets to see are me and the interpreter – and the city's finest.

There's a smirk on his face as we settle ourselves in the small, uncomfortable interview room.

'Nice hotel,' he says through the interpreter.

'You feel like an extended stay?' I retort.

He shrugs. He looks questioningly at Svanhvít, who has taken a seat directly opposite him.

'Let's start with the positive stuff,' I continue. 'The chief superintendent is interested in striking a deal.'

Svanhvít translates for Robertas.

'They believe you're more than just another mule, and that you know both the sellers overseas and the buyers here. You can name names.'

'What are they offering?' he asks.

'He wants the names of your collaborators here, the Icelandic drugs big shots. If it leads to arrests, then there's no doubt it would result in a positive influence on the length of your sentence for smuggling.'

Robertas listens to Svanhvít in silence. Then he asks something and listens to her reply.

'What did he ask?'

'He's wondering how much discount he gets for being a grass.'

'It depends on what information he puts on the table.'

Svanhvít appears to be struggling to explain things. At any rate, Robertas snarls at her.

'What's he getting worked up about?' I ask.

Robertas glares angrily at Svanhvít. When she tries to calm him down, he suddenly slams both hands down on the table.

'What the hell's going on?' I snap.

Robertas focuses on Svanhvít. His words come in a bitter voice.

When she replies to him without translating, I've had enough. I interrupt.

'What did he say just then?'

Her nerves are on edge after the angry exchange with Robertas. Her hands shake as she makes notes in her pad.

'He says he's not prepared to betray his friends,' she says at last.

I get to my feet.

'That's a perfectly clear answer. I'll pass that on.'

Robertas quickly looks up at me, and then at Svanhvít.

He growls a few words with a heavy emphasis to them.

'What did he say?' I repeat.

'I'm not quite sure what he means,' Svanhvít replies awkwardly.

They speak together for a moment.

'Your job is to translate,' I tell her angrily. 'Not to get involved in a long fucking conversation with my client.'

'I'm sorry,' Svanhvít replies. 'He's just cursing everyone and everything for being put in jail. I can translate all the swearing if you like.'

I snatch up my briefcase. I'm heading for the door.

'Come on,' I rasp. 'This conversation is over.'

On the way to the car park, Svanhvít does her best to apologise for herself, and for Robertas.

'I was just trying to calm him down,' she says.

'Really?'

'Robertas has finally realised that he's going to spend years in Litla-Hraun, and that's why he's so angry.'

'First and foremost, he should be angry with himself.'

'Unfortunately, most people prefer to find someone else to blame.'

I take a closer look at Svanhvít. She still seems upset after the exchange with Robertas.

'You look like you need cheering up.'

'Yes. That was something of an ordeal.'

'I'm going to stop in Hveragerði for a coffee. Follow me.'

There's a wonderful secret kept at Hverakaffi on Breiðimörk. It's the most delicious cream cakes in the country. They simply melt in the mouth, triggering every single pleasure synapse in the brain.

Wowww!

They always call to me whenever I have to travel east of the heath. That's even though I know those cakes mean an extra hour in the gym.

They're worth it.

While we enjoy them, I try to fish for Svanhvít's

background. The information has to be dragged out of her, in tiny morsels.

She lived in Lithuania for eight years, initially going there with her father. The old man manages things for a company that's largely owned by one of the Icelandic export gangsters.

Svanhvít studied engineering at university in Vilnius. She still works for her father as an engineer.

'What brought you home?'

'I wanted to be with my mother.'

'Aha.'

'She was diagnosed with cancer two years ago.'

'Sorry to hear it.'

'I'm an only child, so it fell to me to support her.'

'How is she doing in the battle with cancer?'

'She doesn't have long left.'

'I understand.'

'But I'm still working for Dad.'

'Here in Iceland?'

'Yes. But I sometimes go and spend two or three weeks there.'

'So interpreting is just a sideline?

'That's it. There's such a shortage of interpreters.'

We part in the car park, and then my phone sings out.

It's Dagnija.

She's still in Copenhagen.

'New Baltic just gave me a new mobile,' she says.

'That's good.'

'Has Ilona been found?'

'No. But I know who picked her up at El Dorado that night. And I'll keep searching until I find her. You can be sure of that.'

The purring silver steed takes me up and over the heath. Again, I think about the strange conversation between Robertas and Svanhvít. I'm wondering what they were really saying to each other in a language I don't understand.

I'm not sure what to think. I suspect the worst.

As the silver steed approaches the city, I call Lísa Björk to ask when the new interpreter is due to arrive at the office. This is to translate the conversation between the three of us at Litla-Hraun, word for word.

There's a chance that my suspicions are simply an indication that I'm no longer able to trust anyone, that I've lost the capacity to allow anyone the benefit of the doubt. Maybe I'm no longer working on the old fundamental principle of assuming innocence until proven guilty, and all that, in my dealings with other people. That's because of my disappointingly dismal experience of the world of criminals.

A suspicion of evil is the Devil's delight, as Mother said.

22

'The government's on the run from the protests,' Lísa Björk says when I return to the office later that day.

'My prediction is that soon enough those angry cats will devour the confused mice,' I reply.

She's been busy while I was out, collecting information about my new client. That's drug addict Sverrir Guðbjartsson.

He's twenty-six years old. The son of an accountant at Deloitte and a teacher in Mosfellsbær, he's single and childless. For the last few years he's lived in a rented attic flat in an old house on Hverfisgata.

As a teenager he seemed to be going in the right direction. He attended Reykjavík Junior College, following in his father's footsteps. From there he went on to study business at the University of Reykjavík.

That was where things went haywire. His drug habit screwed up his studies. He's twice been in rehab. Both times he was back on the dope a week later.

Lísa Björk's summary shows that Sverrir is a hard-core drug user who lives from one day to the next, and finances his habit by sponging off friends and relatives – and with a bit of theft and burglary.

On the other hand, he has never been accused of using violence.

'He seems to have been a popular guy when he was at college,' Lísa Björk adds. 'It's interesting that his two best friends from that time are now in the police.'

'Do you have names?'

'Glúmur Aðalsteinsson and Eiríkur Egilsson.'

Glúmur and Eiríkur? The pushy pair who picked Ilona up from Porno Valdi's place?

Máki's tongue-in-cheek article mentioning the Bessastaðir security cameras is now online. There's no response from the city's finest.

'I hear other media have been asking about CCTV,' he says. 'But all we get is the standard reply that everything is under investigation.'

Máki has spent decades tailing politicians and villains. He knows better than anyone the dark side of society where politics and money rule the roost behind the scenes, and what takes place in the smoke-filled corridors of power.

'You know all about Benedikt Björgúlfsson's connections, don't you?' I ask.

'It's no secret that he was born an Independence Party member because his father was a city councillor for years,' Máki replies. 'As a student Bensi was deeply into politics and had a seat on the Association of Young Conservatives while he was at university. If my memory's correct, he was on the Association's board along with his pals Gunnar Kjartan, the Reverend Hildibrandur and Bjarni Bjarnason of the Central Bank, and the four of them have always been close allies. I don't know if you saw the interview with the Reverend Hildibrandur in *Morgunblaðið* a few months ago, but there was an old picture there of this gang of four during their university days. They weren't only well known in student politics, but also for their appetite for night life. One friend of theirs tells me that in those years they were young rich, and horny.'

'And the man of God? Was he horny as well?'

'Yep. That was before Hildibrandur found the Lord and switched to theology.'

'Aha.'

'Benedikt was in stocks and shares at the Agricultural Bank, but when it was privatised in the nineties and amalgamated with Kaupthing, Bensi became one of the senior figures at the new bank. He was still running his own share dealing business and was making money hand over fist, including dodgy dealings with shares in DeCode and Oz on the grey market, and back then he managed to convince a load of people to buy these shares at ridiculously pumped up prices. But he never looked back... and raked in the money with non-stop share dealing here and abroad under a whole load of company names. The export Vikings came to him to act as a front for them when they needed to maintain the share prices in their companies that were in fact simply bankrupt.'

'So he must have made a few enemies?'

'You mean ones with enough of a grudge to want to kill him?' Máki asks.

'Uh-huh.'

'I get the impression that plenty of people feel that Bensi got just what he deserved. Take a look at social media. There are a few who want his killer to be made a national hero.'

'And family?'

'Bensi never married and he had no children, but I understand that his sister worked for him as secretary and events manager of some kind, and she survives him. So why the sudden interest in Bensi? You told me that was no concern of yours.'

'Everything is subject to change.'

'What's going on?' the old newshound asks, like a dog at a bone.

'It'll all become clear tomorrow.'

'What?'

'Call me at lunchtime tomorrow.'

Máki doesn't let up, but doesn't get anywhere.

It's not as if I know any more about what the cops are

planning. Fat Raggi refused to supply me with any further information about the evidence against Sverrir Guðbjartsson. That's apart from the candlestick found under the lad's bed, and the testimony of his friend at Bessastaðir.

Late in the afternoon I get hold of her. But that's no help.

'The police say I'm not to discuss this with anyone,' Sveinfríður says, and hangs up.

Rósalind isn't any better. I reach her at around dinner time.

'Don't call me when I'm on duty,' she snaps.

'Hey, take it easy! Your account of events is confirmed.'

'How?'

'I spoke to Sigvaldi.'

'Oh.'

'He admitted that Glúmur and Eiríkur collected Ilona that evening. I'll take that information forward and will indicate Sigvaldi as the source. I thought you ought to know.'

'OK,' Rósalind replies. 'I'll be in touch with you tomorrow.'

It takes me by surprise to see that the TV newshounds have sniffed out the suspicions of the city's finest regarding Sverrir Guðbjartsson. Not that my client is named. At any rate, the TV news states that the police suspect a link between the theft from the Bessastaðir church and the financier's death.

'According to the newsroom's sources, the police are investigating the possibility that the thief had been in the act of stealing these valuable items just as Benedikt Björgúlfsson entered the church, and he then attacked Benedikt, using one of the candlesticks as a weapon,' the newsreader gabbles in excitement. 'While the police consider there is a strong likelihood of the murder being connected to the theft, investigators have not ruled out other potential motives.'

Really?

The news item has the blackbirds' fingerprints all over it. They're obviously clearing the way for a simple explanation for the Bessastaðir murder.

A theft-related murder committed by a junkie is naturally a very welcome way to quell the conspiracy theories that have been all over the internet these last few days. There are endless anonymous assertions about the secret hand of power and corruption that has to be behind Benedikt Björgúlfsson's murder.

It's a simple, easy whitewash job. If they can get away with it.

Unless the wretched boy really is guilty?

23

Tuesday 13th January

It's not just the police who know how to pull media strings.

I sent Inspector Haraldur Haraldsson an email last night. I set out Porno Valdi's testimony, stating that two police officers had collected Ilona from El Dorado the night she disappeared. These are Glúmur Aðalsteinsson and Eiríkur Egilsson. I inquired if there was any reason the police had declined to search for the girl from Latvia.

Then I gave the whole thing to Máki. The story was on the *News Blog* first thing.

Ilona vanished after stripping for cops

Cool headline. That should shake up some of the system's boneheads.

The district court at Lækjartorg is surrounded by photographers and newshounds competing to get a photo of Sverrir in handcuffs.

All the same, the blackbirds have done nothing to prepare the lad for the media frenzy.

He shrinks between them like a frightened mouse. They hustle him through the squawking media crowd and into the court.

'What's all this noise about?' Sverrir asks, his voice shaky as I take a seat next to him.

'These wankers are trying to show the newspapers how smart they are. Bessastaðir murder case wrapped up in less than a week, thank you very much.'

'But I didn't do it.'

'So you say. But they seem to have a full hand of trumps.'

The city's finest want Sverrir under lock and key at Litla-Hraun for an initial six weeks.

After yesterday's interrogation it's no surprise that the prosecutor stresses before the court that the candlestick that was most likely used to beat Benedikt Björgúlfsson to death was found under my client's bed. That was during a search by the blackbirds for drugs in the flat on Hverfisgata on Friday night.

The prosecution application states that according to the pathology report, Benedikt lost his life between four and six in the afternoon on Friday the 2nd of January, and for most of that time my client had certainly been present at Bessastaðir. Analysis confirms that the bloodstains on the candlestick are from the victim. However, samples have been sent for DNA analysis overseas, and results will not be available for some weeks. Mention is also made of blood traces in the boot of the car owned by Sveinfríður Tómasdóttir, which have also been sent for analysis overseas. The court is reminded that Sveinfríður stated that she drove Sverrir home from Bessastaðir shortly after the murder was committed.

The prosecution's lawyer accepts before the court that my client's fingerprints have not been identified on the murder weapon. But he states that this is immaterial, considering the candlestick was found at Sverrir's home. His argument is that if he didn't commit the murder at Bessastaðir himself, he must have been an accessory. For these reasons, it's essential for the investigation that Sverrir remains in isolation for the coming weeks.

I don't have many cards to play in his defence.

First of all there's my client's earnest assertion that he is innocent.

I repeat my demand that recordings from the security cameras at Bessastaðir be placed before the court so that it can be confirmed where precisely Sverrir was at the time of the murder.

The prosecutor replies that the police are still examining the recordings. In the meantime, these will not be made available to others.

It doesn't take the judge long to reach a decision. Without even a break to consider, my client is remanded in custody for four weeks.

I get a chance to speak to Sverrir once the judge has left the court.

'How are you feeling?'

'I had an injection this morning,' he says dully.

He continues to protest his innocence. He's adamant he has no idea how the candlesticks from Bessastaðir ended up under his bed.

'I've never seen these candlesticks,' he says. 'That's the truth.'

'But they were under your bed.'

'I'm not sure about that.'

'Meaning what?'

'They just said they found that shit under my bed and that's all I know about it.'

'Hang on,' I say. 'You didn't witness them finding the candlesticks?'

'No. I was asleep when they came in and started searching.'

'When did you first see these items?'

'That was when they woke me up.'

'And where were the candlesticks then?'

'They were on the floor. One of the cops was putting them in a black sack.'

'You're absolutely sure about this?'

'Yeah. I know what I saw, and what I didn't see.'

Aha.

The cops clap him in handcuffs again. He's led out of the court where a horde of snappers waits to get that one picture.

I accompany Sverrir closely until the blackbirds show him into the van that'll carry him away over the heath, to solitary confinement at Litla-Hraun.

'Is he guilty?' a newshound asks, shoving a microphone into my face.

'Sverrir has from the outset protested his innocence,' I reply.

For a few minutes there's a deluge of questions from the assembled hacks. That's even though every one of them should be aware there's nothing I can add.

'My client is adamant that he is innocent of this crime,' I repeat. 'I consider it proper to make no further comment until I have had an opportunity to examine and evaluate the prosecution's potential evidence.'

Then I march along Austurstræti. I fancy soup at Café Paris. But as soon as I hear the racket from Austurvöllur, I head along Pósthússtræti.

There's a group of protestors in front of the Parliament building, where a cluster of nervous blackbirds are on duty. Men and women shout the 'incompetent government' slogan. They're banging pots, pans and other metal items to make sure their point reaches those inside the seat of power. Others wave homemade placards demanding ministers resign, and calling for immediate elections.

A hundred days have passed since the banks collapsed, without a single politician or official resigning. Our slow-witted Prime Minister holds on tight to the reins of power at the cabinet offices on Lækjargata. The banking minister hasn't stepped down. Let alone the foreign minister who made it this amateur government's chief aim for Iceland to claim a seat on the United Nations Security Council. This was all after the privatised Icelandic banks turned into a scorched earth machine that would sooner or later blow the country up.

Protestors crowd around the black ministerial limousines that cruise up to Parliament. The blackbirds try to push them back. They form a cordon around the cars, then escort the ministers inside.

A barrage of abuse rains over them the whole time.

I'm making for the statue of Jón Sigurðsson, the hero of Iceland's independence. That's when I see Freyja Dögg among the cluster of protestors.

'Are you here to protest with us?' she demands eagerly.

'No,' I smile.

Her cheeks are pink. There's a burning passion in her eyes.

'I'm not giving up until these arseholes have all resigned,' she gasps. She points at Parliament.

'All the same, be careful. Because of your arm.'

'Y'know, my mother is livid,' Freyja Dögg continues with delight. 'She's been trying to get me to drop the charges because the guy who ran me down is an old family friend.'

'Really?'

'Yep. But I'm taking no notice of her bullshit.'

'Good for you. You should always follow your heart, first and last.'

'Fucking right!'

Freyja Dögg is on her feet as another limousine pulls up outside Parliament. The same furious slogan about an incompetent minister. It's delivered with the enviable conviction and sincerity of youth.

Time never fails to douse the fires of passion, as Mother said.

24

Always being right is a real pain in the arse.

A precise translation by new interpreter Thuríður Jónasdóttir of the conversation between me, Robertas and Svanhvít at Litla-Hraun yesterday confirms my suspicions.

Svanhvít wasn't just translating for me, as she was required to. She was also passing messages to my client. That includes clear and direct threats.

She was partly speaking obliquely. All the same, Robertas didn't seem to have any difficulty understanding what she was driving at. And he didn't take kindly to what she had to say.

I go through the conversation again, word by word. I'm trying to figure out what this pair are plotting, the court interpreter and the drugs mule.

There are two sections that are particularly interesting. The first starts just after I explained the city's finest's offer of co-operation.

Robertas: What happens if I tell them everything they want to know?'

Svanhvít: You know what'll happen. That's out of my hands.

Stella: What did he ask?

Svanhvít: He's wondering how much discount he gets for being a grass.'

Thuríður's translated transcript makes it abundantly clear that Svanhvít lied to me − bare-faced − and kept it up through the rest of our conversation.

Svanhvít: I thought you knew exactly what you're supposed to do.

Robertas: Then why make threats?'

Svanhvít: They want to be certain that you'll keep your side of the bargain.

Robertas: Where is she?

Svanhvít: In a safe place.

Robertas: That's a double cross! A stab in the back.

Stella: What's he getting worked up about?

Svanhvít: Calm down, will you? Before she gets suspicious.

Robertas bangs hard on the table.

Stella: What the hell's going on?

Robertas: Don't forget that I can also get my own back.

Svanhvít: Not while you're in here.

Stella: What did he say just then?

Svanhvít: He says he's not prepared to betray his friends.

Stella: That's a perfectly clear answer. I'll pass that on.

Robertas: If anything happens to her, I'll be coming after you.

Stella: What did he say?

Svanhvít: I'm not quite sure what he means.

The lying bitch.

I'm livid that she abused my trust on such a scale – and made threats against my client. Un-be-fucking-lievable!

And on whose behalf was she lying? Maybe more than one person?

All the indications are that Svanhvít is in cahoots with the foreign criminals who put the dope in the BMW. At any rate, there's no more plausible explanation that comes to mind for her reprehensible conduct.

I read through two sentences in particular.

Robertas: Where is she?

Svanhvít: In a safe place.

The implication is that Svanhvít's bosses overseas are holding captive a woman who's dear to Robertas. That's no doubt to ensure he doesn't speak too freely to the guardians of law and order. A girlfriend? A sister? His mother?

I'm on my feet. I get myself an ink-black coffee from the Nespresso machine.

What the hell am I going to do?'

After a moment's thought I call Lísa Björk, the clever chick who has already read the transcripts. She understands my predicament.

'As a covert recording of a conversation with a client is a clear breach of legal protocol, you'll need to find some strategy to use this information, but without indicating how it was obtained,' she says.

'Just...'

'The simplest option is to do nothing.'

I mull it over.

'Apart from that, you'll have to ensure that Svanhvít doesn't get to meet Robertas again.'

'But she's the cops' interpreter.'

'Yes, and that makes this even more serious. In fact, I find it hard to believe that they didn't investigate her background in detail before allowing her to translate for these men.'

'I'll have to find a way to expose that lying bitch.'

'How?'

'The first step is to speak to Robertas again. I need him to open up.'

She shakes her blonde head.

'If there's anything in these threats, which seem to be serious, then I don't believe he'll tell you a thing. He's undoubtedly too frightened to say anything.'

'Anyway, I have to try. Would you check with Thuríður when she's free to go out east with me?'

'No problem.'

Lísa Björk hands me a slip of paper, with two names, addresses and phone numbers. These are the names Jörundur Hákonarson gave me the other day when I called on him at Sunnuhlíð.

'They're both alive and mentally alert,' she says. 'Eygló Arnardóttir, the former housekeeper at Hvítanes, lives in Bíldudalur but she'll be arriving here in Reykjavík next week. She said she has to travel south for a hip replacement at the National Hospital and she has a room at the Red Cross hostel for ten days.'

'That's handy.'

'Former bank manager Hermann Rögnvaldsson lives in Fljótshlíð, on a farm he bought about fifteen years ago,' she continues 'He's reputed to be short-tempered and difficult, especially with strangers. I spoke to an old friend of his, who reckons it's out of the question that Hermann would be prepared to discuss family affairs with you.'

'We'll see.'

He's a grumpy heavyweight powerbroker who's accustomed to getting his own way. As cantankerous as hell in his old age. Just like that old grouch Egill Skallagrímsson.

I'm already looking forward to taking on this disagreeable old bastard.

25

The cops grill Sverrir Guðbjartsson well into the evening.

They're after a precise, detailed account of everything he did from the moment he woke up around midday on Friday the 2nd of January up to when the boys in black shoved their way into his place roughly a week later. That's easier said than done, considering my client's life seems to take place mostly in a drugged haze. At least, he says he doesn't remember where he was or what he was doing for whole days at a time.

But it's the events of that Friday that are crucial.

Sverrir thinks he woke up around one, and went downtown to look up some acquaintances who might be able to help him score.

He admits having got hold of enough to give himself a lift, but reckons he doesn't remember where or in whose company. Not that any of us are inclined to believe that.

Around three on the Friday he called Sveinfríður Tómasdóttir who told him she would finish work at Bessastaðir between four and five. He hitched a ride out to Álftanes shortly before four. He claims not to know who the driver was, but that he got out at the end of the road leading up to Bessastaðir. From there he had to walk up to the church by the President's residence.

Sveinfríður was still busy when he got there. She let him wait in her car, handing him the keys so he could open it.

Sverrir's tale is that he lay down on the back seat and

went to sleep.

This is the tale he sticks to all through the day. He's adamant that he was still asleep when his friend finished work.

While Sveinfríður's account also states that Sverrir was in the back of the car when she got behind the wheel, it doesn't mention him being asleep.

The cops consider my client's narrative to be a pack of lies. They go back and forth through their theories about the theft of the candlesticks, Benedikt Björgúlfsson's murder and Sverrir's presumed part in all this. But he's having none of it, and sticks firmly to his account.

After a few hours of to and fro, I repeat my demand that the footage from the security cameras at Bessastaðir be made available.

'These recordings must show clearly whether or not my client is telling the truth,' I say. 'It's his absolute right to have access to these images.'

'They're still being evaluated,' fat Raggi says sulkily.

'Badgering my client without producing the only evidence that would presumably confirm what happened during that critical hour is indefensible.'

The city's finest take no notice of me. They continue to push Sverrir from pillar to post and back. But it's hopeless.

In fact, it took me by surprise that my client was able to stand up to this pressure. My experience as a lawyer dealing with a great many junkies has been very different. Their testimony tends to flutter all over the place like leaves in the wind.

'There's something more than a little spooky about this CCTV,' I say as the interrogation ends. 'I'll be presenting my demand for this before the district court.'

'That's your right,' Raggi says drily.

Back at the office, Lísa Björk gives me some startling news of the Ilona case.

'The Reykjavík police force has issued a statement just

now,' she says. 'They're accusing you and Máki of spreading falsehoods.'

Right away, I call Máki, who's worried.

'The cops are demanding that I withdraw the story about the strip show at the police college, and issue an apology,' he says. 'Who's fooling who?'

'Take it easy,' I tell him. 'What does it say in their statement?'

'Just that the force absolutely rejects the claims made by *News Blog* that police officers collected Ilona from El Dorado on the evening of her disappearance,' Máki replies.

'On what grounds?'

'They quote a statement by Sigvaldi Auðólfsson, who denies having identified police officers in connection with Ilona's disappearance during a conversation with you,' Máki continues. 'His assistant, Jónsteinn Ingólfsson, who was present at your meeting at El Dorado, corroborates Sigvaldi's statement. The cops demand a retraction, and they say they're going to pull you up before the Bar Council's ethics committee.'

'Fuck, what a load of wank.'

Máki sighs.

'It's beyond belief that the cops are daring to rely on false statements from Porno Valdi and Jónsteinn,' I add.

'Can you prove it?'

'Not for the moment. But everything that's in your story is correct and true.'

'OK. In that case I'll stand by it,' Máki replies. 'I've faced worse.'

Rósalind sent me a text message earlier in the day. We arrange to meet at Öskjuhlíð, where quiet pathways meander through the woods.

She's wearing the dark jogging gear, and chunky running shoes.

The beautiful red hair frames her face.

'There's chaos at the station, thanks to you,' she says.

'Haraldur had Porno Valdi brought in in a squad car, and Jónsteinn as well.'

'And he got them to lie?'

'I don't believe he's that dishonest.'

'You think it's more likely he believes their lies?'

'I reckon that's the way it has to be,' Rósalind replies. 'I know Haraldur still hasn't raised this with Glúmur or Eiríkur, or any of us who were at the party at the police college that night, and my feeling is that this means Sigvaldi hasn't named any names.'

'It's as fishy as hell.'

'Haraldur believes obsessively that you're running a campaign to slander the police.'

'You know better.'

'Yes, but I no longer have any proof.'

I take hold of her shoulders.

'We have to find Ilona before it's too late.'

'Yes, I agree completely.'

I'm lost in those seductive deep-green eyes.

Rósalind gasps slightly as I move aside a lock of red hair from her cheek. But she doesn't look away. Instinctively, she moistens her lips with the tip of her tongue.

It's an offer that's too good to refuse.

26

The Reykjavík blackbirds' counter-offensive is plastered across all of that evening's news bulletins. There's a short statement from me. I stand by every word.

But how am I going to prove it all?

When we parted on Öskjuhlíð, I warned Rósalind to be cautious. That's despite having previously told her to report to her superiors what she had seen at the police college that night.

Now I need to try other options.

Rósalind mentioned that she'd had an idea, but didn't want to say any more at this point. She wanted to be sure it would work.

Sandra Ósk Sigurgeirsdóttir calls just before eight. She's the mother of Freyja Dögg, the activist with her arm in a sling.

Right up to the financial crash, Sandra Ósk was one of the country's most popular politicians, according to media polls. That's even though she practically inherited her seat in Parliament from her father. He had been a well-known footballer in his younger days, but took instead to mixing business with pleasure once he'd hung up his football boots. He became rich and powerful within the party that has called the shots in Iceland for the last half-century. Until his heart gave out five years ago.

'It was Gunnar Kjartan who gave the green light for Sandra Ósk to step into the old man's shoes,' Máki related.

'He also supported her dad during his political career. They were close friends.'

That's Gunnar Kjartan Vestmann, childhood friend of Benedikt Björgúlfsson. This is the wealthy powerbroker my newshound friend says has been the cornerstone of Iceland's power class for the last couple of decades, all the way back to the eighties.

'Anyone he's supported has done well for themselves, either within the party or the establishment,' Máki said. 'I could also give you the names of plenty of decent people who were cast into political exile after falling out with Gunnar Kjartan. That's a political death sentence.'

Sandra's nowhere near as popular since the financial crash. She's paying the price of her husband's actions, as he was one of the bigwigs at Kaupthing until it folded. Hrólfur was also one of the owners and managers of the Icelandic banks who did a moonlight flit in private jets to London with suitcases stuffed with pounds, dollars, euros and Swiss francs, cleaning out every scrap of paper money they could lay their hands on as the banks capsized.

The bulging suitcases were naturally just small change compared to the billions that the owners and managers of these banks shovelled out of the doors in the weeks and months leading up to the crash. All the same, the managers fleeing the country with stacks of cash became emblematic in the general public's eyes of the bank job of the millennium.

Over the last few weeks Sandra Ósk has found out that being married to a bank robber isn't a ticket to being popular with voters. Not even in Iceland.

All the same, she comes across as the one calling the shots.

'My opinion is that as a lawyer, you should be talking some sense into Freyja Dögg instead of encouraging her to pursue hopeless litigation,' she says without any preamble.

I decide to stay cool.

'You should be aware after eighteen years of acquaintance with your daughter that Freyja Dögg has a mind of her own,' I reply.

'On the contrary, she's very easily led,' Sandra Ósk says. 'Otherwise she wouldn't be taking part in these idiotic protests, organised by anarchists and communists.'

'Politics isn't my department.'

'I demand that you withdraw this lawsuit.'

'It's Freyja Dögg who's doing this, not me. You'll have to speak to her.'

'I know you're behind this,' Sandra Ósk rages. 'Do you think I don't know that you're constantly agitating against the police and authorities?'

'As far as I'm aware, Freyja Dögg is an adult. She has every right to make her own decisions.'

'You know perfectly well that it was nothing more than an accident. This lawsuit is only going to cause more trouble for Freyja Dögg.'

'The images we have indicate that this was no accident, and this was a deliberate act by the driver of the vehicle.'

'I'm telling you that the person who'll be hurt the most if this lawsuit isn't withdrawn is Freyja Dögg herself.'

'How so?'

'She'll be charged with illegal protest and an assault on the Central Bank.'

'I imagine you're joking.'

'No,' Sandra Ósk snaps. 'I'm fully aware that the police will take this seriously and will more than likely charge Freyja Dögg with a serious offence against the authorities. That's why I want you to withdraw this lawsuit.'

By now I've had enough.

'Shouldn't you be supporting your daughter rather than being her adversary?' I ask, voice sharp. I'm not hiding my anger.

'I'm trying to help her, but she won't listen to me, thanks to all the bad advice she gets from the insane people she mainly spends her time with these days. I'm convinced that if you advise her to withdraw the charges, she would agree.'

'I reckon that's unlikely.'

'I demand that you make an effort to get her to behave sensibly in this matter.'

'Look. I've met your daughter on two occasions. Both times she was very certain and knew precisely what she wanted to do. All I've done is to bring her grievance to the attention of the correct authorities.'

'Freyja Dögg is a silly girl who's easily led. I know all about that.'

'I'll certainly inform her that she can expect to be served with a lawsuit from Bjarni Bjarnason at the Central Bank and will find out how she wants to respond. But it'll be entirely her decision, not mine.'

'I'm relying on you to talk sense into her,' Sandra Ósk says, and bangs down the phone.

Sheesh!

When Sóley Árdís has fallen asleep, I stretch out on the soft sofa in the living room. I treat myself to a generous Jack D, the sweet nectar of Tennessee. I close my eyes. My thoughts go back to the woods on Öskjuhlíð. I can feel Rósalind's sweet lips on mine.

The thought has my heart hammering in my chest. It's like being in love for the first time, all over again.

The honey sweetness of love is a delusion, as Mother said.

27

Wednesday 14th January

Lísa Björk sits next to my desk with her little laptop in her lap.

'There's a new problem concerning Ásthildur,' she says.

'What now?'

'The statistics authority has her listed as deceased.'

'Deceased? When?'

'According to the national database, she died on 25th October 1972, the same day that her mother drowned.'

This information certainly comes as a surprise. It's completely at odds with Hákon Hákonarson's assertions – and the testimony of his brother Jörundur.

Or...?

Lísa Björk looks up from the screen.

'There's no record anywhere else of Ásthildur's death at the same time as her mother's,' she continues. 'According to newspaper records from October 1972, Hjördís Eyjólfsdóttir's body was found on the shore near Grótta on Seltjarnarnes. There's no mention of Ásthildur. Ten days later there's a death notice in *Morgunblaðið* placed by Hjördís's parents. It states that her funeral has taken place in private, and there's no mention of her daughter.'

'Which indicates that the death information held by the statistics authority is false.'

'Could be.'

'Jörundur warned me specifically about this possibility. He believed it likely that in 1972 Hermann Rögnvaldsson ensured that there were no official records anywhere in the system relating to whatever became of Ásthildur.'

Lísa Björk nods. She looks down again at the little screen.

'I heard from Thuríður Jónasdóttir yesterday evening,' she says. 'She can go out east with you this afternoon or tomorrow.'

'Bad shit's best got over with.'

Thuríður is well over sixty.

Back in the seventies she met a young Nordic studies student from Lithuania at the University of Iceland. They married and went to live in Vilnius when his studies were completed. Once there, she learned the language, and taught Icelandic and Nordic literature at university. When her husband passed away eight years ago, she returned to Iceland. Since then she has worked as a court interpreter and further education teacher.

We meet at Litla-Hraun at two. She's a petite, delicate woman with fair hair and a colourful scarf around her neck. She's wrapped in a thick, warm winter coat, and wearing black winter boots.

Robertas is more agitated than at our meeting last week.

'He's asking after Svanhvít,' Thuríður says.

'She has other business to attend to.'

My reply takes Robertas by surprise. He looks at me questioningly.

'You'll have to tell me honestly what's going on,' I tell him. 'If you want me to try and help you.'

Thuríður translates my words for him.

'He asks what you are talking about.'

'I know you have been threatened,' I say.

Robertas shrugs.

'I also know that those threatening you are holding someone close to you. And that they use Svanhvít as a messenger.'

He stares at me.

'What can I do to help you find a solution to this?' I ask.

Robertas sits motionless and silent for some time. His face is as still as if it's frozen.

'Nothing,' he replies at last.

'The police are ready to co-operate. Both here and in Lithuania.'

Thuríður translates his short reply.

'No. Too dangerous.'

'Do you know who's giving Svanhvít instructions?'

Robertas is silent. He's expressionless. He just stares at me. I try repeatedly to get him to open up. But no success.

'Well, then,' I say and get to my feet. 'If you change your mind, let me know. I can come and see you at short notice if required.'

Thuríður and I walk together across the car park in front of the prison.

'This doesn't come as a surprise, all this about Svanhvít,' she says.

'You know her?'

'We've met a few times at Lithuanian gatherings here in Reykjavík,' Thuríður replies. 'But I hear that she has friends among people who have repeatedly been at odds with the law, both here and abroad.'

I stop between our cars.

'Could you name names?

'It's not my role to accuse anyone of illegal activity,' she replies. 'On the other hand, the National Police Commissioner's office has the names of all these men in its records, as the police carefully watch what these men get up to.'

'But without arresting any of them?'

'The police need to have witnesses and people are very frightened of these men. They are ruthless, as they have shown in the past, and don't hesitate to administer brutal beatings. Taking a stand against these villains isn't a decision to be taken lightly, let alone bearing witness against them in court.'

Thuríður looks up, her face grave.

'I understand perfectly well why Robertas is reluctant to inform on these men if their friends in Lithuania are holding a relative of his captive,' she adds. 'Those who get in the way of organised crime in Lithuania tend to vanish without trace.'

I sit for a while behind the silver steed's wheel before starting the engine. I'm frustrated that I haven't been able to get Robertas to trust me.

Giving up isn't an option.

Certainly not.

I need to take sensible decisions about the next step – consider whether it's time to apply pressure to Svanhvít.

28

My silver steed purrs with contentment on the road leading east to Fljótshlíð. The snow-clad peaks of brooding volcanoes jut skywards: Hekla, Katla, Eyjafjallajökull.

Lines of verse learned by heart to be publicly recited during college years at Laugarvatn surface from deep in my memory.

Ice at the peaks, fires burning beneath.

The Merc takes the occasional patch of ice on the grey tarmac in its stride. It's like a supernatural chariot of the gods who were once worshipped in these parts. That was the time when the heroes of Njál's Saga competed to slaughter as many as possible of each other in their thirst for fame, wealth and women.

When heroes rode through these fields, as the old-fashioned romantic poet put it back in the old days. Of course, that was long before Iceland's wealthiest decided that Fljótshlíð was theirs for the taking. They've filled it with stock exchange-style summer houses.

A decade and a half ago Hermann Rögnvaldsson bought a piece of land with a famous name in what used to be contented countryside. Now a very elderly man, he's said to spend most of his time there.

I surprised myself in the car park at Litla-Hraun. I took a spur-of-the-moment decision to call on the old guy, to press him for answers to my questions about Ásthildur's fate.

Hermann's had a new house built on the rise where the old farmhouse once was. This fashionable homage to Mammon is all glass and steel.

The thick curtains of the living room are pulled shut. But there's a glistening black 4x4 parked in front of the shut garage doors. That's an indication the old man is home.

I park the silver steed beside the Range Rover. I ring the doorbell a few times, until the old guy finally answers the door.

He's on the short side, and chubby. His hair's grey, his face fat, eyes small and sharp. His nose curves like the beak of a bird of prey.

'We're not buying anything,' he says in a hoarse voice and slams the door.

I press the button again. More than once. Until he opens the door again.

'What the hell's going on?' he asks. 'Do you want me to call the police?'

'I'm not selling anything,' I reply, handing him my card.

Hermann fishes a pair of glasses from the pocket of his pale grey cardigan. He peers at the card.

'You're telling me you're a lawyer?' he asks, pocketing his glasses.

'I'd like to ask you a few questions about Ásthildur Ásvaldsdóttir.'

The old man's eyes narrow.

'Never heard of her,' he says in a dry tone.

'I'm sure you must recall your only grandchild.'

Hermann's face flushes.

'You impertinent bitch,' he rages. 'How dare you intrude in my home and stick your nose into my personal affairs?'

'I just need answers to a few questions.'

The old geezer's breath comes in fast gasps.

'I thought the obvious thing would be to ask you first,' I add with a smile. 'Before asking other people.'

'What other people?'

'The officials who helped you falsify Ásthildur's death certificate in October 1972.'

'You must be an extraordinarily foolish woman if you reckon you're not only a lawyer but also a medium,' he sneers. 'I was always opposed to allowing women to join the bar, for good reasons.'

'The truth about Ásthildur will come out, regardless of what you think,' I reply placidly. 'Giving you an opportunity to justify your actions seemed the right thing to do.'

'Justify!' Hermann hisses. 'There's not a single thing I need to justify!'

'Do you think your grandchild will agree with that when...'

'I have no grandchild,' he interrupts.

'...when I find Ásthildur and give her an account of how you treated her mother?'

'Hjördís was a disgusting whore who wrecked my sons' lives.'

'The truth is quite the opposite. They ruined her life.'

'You're talking nonsense, as all women do. It was this wretched whore of Babylon who led my sons to their deaths.'

'That's not what I've been hearing.'

'My boys studied diligently in Copenhagen until they fell for that witch. Hjördís tempted them with drugs and perverted sex, and that was the ruin of them. She alone bore responsibility for their deaths.'

I look Hermann up and down.

'So why take out your spite on your innocent grandchild?'

'The child wasn't Ásvaldur's,' he snaps. 'I could see immediately from the look of the girl, and the whore of Babylon admitted as much to me on the day I buried my sons.'

'I see. So that's why you arranged for the Child

Protection Committee to take Ásthildur from her mother. Which led to Hjördís taking her own life. Check and mate.'

'The whore finally felt some guilt and did what she was supposed to do,' he replies. 'Justice was served.'

'You still believe that? After all these years?'

Hermann puts his hands to his chest.

'What became of Ásthildur?' I ask.

'You've sapped enough of my strength,' he replies. 'Get off my property before I call the District Commissioner in Hvolsvöllur, who's a good friend of mine, and have you arrested.'

'Watch your ticker,' I say. 'I'd prefer it if you don't keel over until I'm gone.'

I get behind the wheel. The silver steed hurtles down the steep slope and I wrench the car onto the main road. Time to head west.

On the way to Reykjavík I think over Hjördís's miserable end.

She never had a chance, from the moment she was in this arrogant bastard's sights. He clearly got a kick out of abusing his powers.

The revenge of this old, bitter loner in his glass palace was cruel. But after having met the old man, I doubt that his revenge gave him the satisfaction he craved.

Revenge is sweet, but it heals no hurts, as Mother said.

29

Thursday 15th January

'We're going to start a riot on Tuesday,' Freyja Dögg says earnestly.

'Why wait until then?' I ask with a smile.

'That's when Parliament returns for the first session of the year and these fucking idiots are going to be met with such a racket and a fuss that they'll have to resign.'

'Presumably you know that Icelandic politicians never, ever, resign due to poor judgement in their work. Taking responsibility for their own mistakes is something that's simply missing from their genetic make-up.'

'We're not giving up until this administration steps down,' she replies. 'Even if we have to surround Parliament for a hundred days.'

This morning Bjarni Bjarnason's lawyer filed a lawsuit against Freyja Dögg for having illegally hindered his client from going about his lawful business on the Central Bank's premises. He's also having her charged with threatening the security of the state by interrupting the business of the Central Bank, which plays a vital role in ensuring the nation's financial security. He's demanding the heaviest sentence the law allows.

Before that, Freyja Dögg had again refused her mother's entreaty to withdraw her own lawsuit and to reach a settlement with the Central Bank guy.

'I don't give a shit that this Bjarni is a friend of hers,' she said this morning. 'I'm not giving way until he's been found guilty of deliberately running me down. Shitbags like that belong behind bars.'

Freyja Dögg is young and lively, full of optimism and spoiling for a fight.

I almost envy her.

The cops seem as nervous as hell these days. At any rate, they're mightily displeased with the demand I put before the District Court this week for access to all of the CCTV footage from Bessastaðir on Friday the 2nd of January.

I made the point before the court that twelve days have passed since Benedikt Björgúlfsson's body was found. That should be more than long enough for the police to evaluate the recordings from the security cameras. I told them it's wrong that my client is being held on remand without either his defence lawyer or the judge having been able to see this crucial evidence. This could establish beyond doubt whether my client entered the church at Bessastaðir or not.

The blackbirds' response is pathetic. They repeat that it's completely inappropriate at this juncture for the suspect or his lawyer to have access to the footage, and that the police expect to be allowed the necessary time to complete their investigation.

No doubt they know perfectly well how weak this argument is.

Máki's up early and gets straight to the point.

'Have you seen Bensi's autopsy report?' he asks.

'No. Why?'

'One of my cop pals told me last night that something was found on the body that they can't explain,' Máki says.

'What's that?'

'He didn't know, but I was wondering if it had appeared in the autopsy report.'

'They're keeping all the documentation to themselves. Playing it close to the chest.'

'My contact also said that they're convinced Sverrir committed the murder in the church,' Máki adds. 'From their point of view, the case is cut and dried, but someone on the investigation team isn't happy with loose ends.'

Fat Raggi calls that afternoon. He's trying to avoid a court hearing about the Bessastaðir footage.

'Can't we reach an agreement about these recordings?' he asks.

'If I get to see them,' I shoot back.

'There's nothing there to be seen.'

'So why keep it secret?'

'Well, the thing is that the security system at Bessastaðir is pretty old. Recordings are still on video tape. That's why it's so time-consuming for our people to go through them.'

'I don't see why it's taking you so long to check recordings that are no use,' I tell him.

'I'm expecting to get the experts' report at the weekend,' Raggi continues. 'Once that's available, there's no obstacle to you having copies of the recordings.'

'On Monday?'

'Monday or Tuesday.'

That's four days. Five at the most.

It's a decent offer under the circumstances. It'll no doubt take longer than that to push my demand through the District Court and then the Supreme Court. That's if the judgements are in my favour, which is by no means certain.

'What about other case files?' I ask.

'What about them?'

'I need to have copies of all the reports relating to Sverrir's case. That includes the pathologist's autopsy report.'

This guardian of law and order is silent for a moment.

'The autopsy report hasn't been made available to us officially, and it won't be for at least a week,' he replies at last.

'Was there anything on Benedikt Björgúlfsson's laptop that sheds any light on his murder?'

Raggi hesitates again.

'We didn't find a laptop.'

'No laptop?'

'No.'

'A laptop-less export Viking? Pull the other one.'

'We've searched Benedikt's home, his office and his car.'

'The police reports must be available by now?'

'Yes, sure. You should be able to get copies of those before the weekend, but that depends on you retracting the lawsuit at the District Court.'

'All right.'

I'm deep in the financial reorganisation of the Stella Fund when Lísa Björk comes in with unwelcome news of the old lady out west, Eygló Arnardóttir.

'The National Hospital has postponed her operation indefinitely,' she says.

'Why's that?'

'They're required to reduce expenditure more this year than last, so all sorts of surgical procedures scheduled for next month have been postponed.'

'So they're cutting back instead up slicing up?'

Lísa Björk smiles wanly.

'There's no certainty that Eygló will be travelling south next week, as had been planned.'

'Hell!'

'She said she doesn't feel comfortable discussing these things on the phone, and asked if you would come and see her in Bíldudalur?'

'It takes at least two days to run out there to the edge of the world?'

'And you might be weather-bound, so it could easily eat up a week.'

Sheesh!

As if I don't have enough on my plate.

30

The afternoon sun casts the long shadow of the white Grótta lighthouse over the boulder-strewn shoreline. Crystal fingers of ice hang like shards of glass from the weed that clings to the largest rocks.

An elderly couple make their gradual way along the beige and black strip of shingle that connects the uninhabited island with Seltjarnarnes. The track will be covered before evening by the rising tide.

Cloak-and-dagger isn't my style.

But Rósalind doesn't dare meet me at my office. Nothing I could say over the phone would persuade her to change her mind. That's why I'm waiting here in the cold.

She runs along the tarmac path that lies just above the tideline. She's wearing a black jogging outfit, red hair hidden under a dark hat.

Rósalind halts at my side. She extends her arms and legs as if she's stretching. Imperceptibly, a little white memory stick is handed to me.

'What's this?'

'I went to every one of the shops near El Dorado,' she replies. 'Five of them have CCTV outside. One of these covers the pavement all the way as far as the night club.'

'And?'

'The shop's owner let me have a copy of the recording for 27th December. The sequences confirm what I told you, that Glúmur and Eiríkur fetched Ilona there that night.'

'Brilliant!'

I tuck the memory stick away in the pocket of my red-brown leather jacket.

Rósalind gives me a quick glance. Her face shows the tension and her concern.

'You can use that to apply some pressure on Haraldur. But absolutely no mention of my name.'

She quickly turns away. Without another word, she jogs back the way she came.

I hurry to get out of the cold, get the silver steed going. I head along the coast and back into Reykjavík, where I plug the stick into the computer.

The CCTV sequence is around a minute. It's date- and time-stamped.

I watch it a couple of times. Then I freeze it at the point showing the clearest image. It shows Glúmur Aðalsteinsson and Eiríkur Egilsson by the jeep's open door. Ilona is there between them. It's timed 22.56.32 on 27th December 2008.

Copper-bottomed proof.

When I arrive at the station at Hlemmur, Haraldur pretends to be busy. But I'm not giving up until he agrees to meet me for a couple of minutes at reception.

'There's no peace from you,' he grumbles.

I hand him a CD in a white envelope.

'Is this an apology?'

'Quite the opposite,' I tell him frostily. 'This is evidence that two police officers collected Ilona from El Dorado a few minutes before eleven o'clock on 27th December.'

He's stunned.

'What sort of evidence?'

'In addition, it demonstrates that this ridiculous statement of yours accusing myself and *News Blog* of peddling untruths is a pack of lies.'

Haraldur rips the envelope open.

'What sort of evidence?' he repeats.

'CCTV footage. It shows Glúmur and Eiríkur with Ilona between them. Standing next to Glúmur's Land Cruiser.'

'Where's the original?'

'It's your choice whether this appears on *News Blog* tomorrow morning,' I continue, ignoring the question. 'On top of that, I ought to have you charged with dereliction of duty.'

This blackbird's calmed down a little now. He turns the CD over in his hands.

'I need to ... let's see ... examine this in detail,' he says at last.

'Then don't let me keep you,' I say shortly, and head for the door.

Haraldur calls that evening.

'There's an announcement going this evening, asking for information relating to Ilona,' he says without preamble.

'About time.'

'Glúmur and Eiríkur have admitted they fetched the girl from El Dorado that evening, as the pictures show, but they are both adamant that she got a lift back with someone else,' he continues. 'We're now checking three CCTV cameras around the police college in the hope that we can find what happened to her.'

'Any success?'

'Nothing so far. But we've just got started.'

'And I imagine the accusations against me and Máki will be withdrawn?'

'That's on the Commissioner's desk right now.'

Haraldur is worried sick that pictures are going to show up on *News Blog*.

'It could affect the investigation if this appears online,' he says.

'If there's a suitable correction and an apology from the Commissioner, then no doubt Máki and I will be prepared to consider the situation,' I say coldly. 'But we both have good reasons to vigorously defend our reputations and professional integrity.'

That evening I call Dagnija. She's still in Copenhagen. I tell her the police are searching, at last.

'I just hope it's not too late,' she says.

Otherwise, Dagnija sounds cheerful.

'The agency let me have a room and a phone,' she says. 'But I'm so worried about Ilona.'

'Does her family know that she's being searched for?'

'I spoke to her mother, and she knows nothing of what Ilona is doing,' Dagnija replies. 'Nor her boyfriend, as he's in prison.'

'She has a boyfriend in prison?'

'Yes. He's been really unlucky.'

'Unlucky?'

'Yeah. Ilona was hoping to meet him in Reykjavík, but he was arrested for some gear that was in his car.'

I'm taken by surprise. Now I'm seeing Ilona's disappearance in a new light.

'Who's Ilona's boyfriend?' I ask, to get my suspicion confirmed.

'His name's Robertas and he's from Lithuania,' Dagnija replies.

31

Friday 16th January

There's a whole double-page spread in *Morgunblaðið* dedicated to Benedikt Björgúlfsson.

Most of the recollections of him seem to be written by old friends and relatives. As well as those, one low-rent politician and two past their sell-by date banking mandarins have also found themselves compelled to put pen to paper to list the murdered man's achievements.

Are wealthy playboys with reputations in ruins still Iceland's heroes?

Although I can't be bothered to read through all these eulogies, my eye stops at a contribution from the surviving three of the gang of four, where Gunnar Kjartan, Bjarni Bjarnason and the Reverend Hildibrandur recollect their joyful youth. That was when they were all on their journey through the Reykjavík Junior College and then the law faculty of the University of Iceland. Plus there was the city's night life. And there was the city's Association of Young Conservatives.

Gunnar Kjartan and Bjarni Bjarnason write fawningly of how Benedikt Björgúlfsson became filthy rich in no time at all, like others of his generation and way of thinking.

They try their utmost to convince readers that with their actions and by amassing wealth over the last decade, these guys have first and foremost been toiling on behalf of the people of Iceland. Not for themselves.

These are the proud standard-bearers of deception, and of the dead and buried Icelandic financial system.

Some people will never learn what shame is.

The priest's words are soused in a reluctant nostalgia for the innocence of youth, otherwise expressed through lofty philosophical meanderings about earthly sin, repentance and forgiveness.

Or is the Reverend Hildibrandur referring to his own sins? Or the sins of the friend to whom he's saying farewell? Or is he simply whining out loud, as these paper priests do?

It's not clear.

Máki calls at lunchtime. He's desperate to tell me about Benedikt's funeral, which has just taken place in Reykjavík's cathedral.

'The place was packed,' he says. 'The entire *crème de la crème* of the disgraced financial sector was there. The only thing missing was Elton John singing for them!'

Máki laughs uproariously at his own comment.

Late last night the blackbirds sent out a press release concerning Ilona's disappearance. They urge anyone who might know anything about the Latvian girl's movements on and after 27th December to get in touch with the police.

But there's no sign of an apology. The city's Commissioner of Police still hasn't retracted the force's serious accusations against me and Máki.

The old newshound's spoiling for a fight.

'I want that picture of Glúmur and Ilona on *News Blog* as soon as poss,' he says.

'Let's see what the day brings,' I say.

'I don't like to sit on something that's dynamite.'

'You know I'm not one to shy away from a fight. But it would be best for us if they withdraw their accusations. Then you can publish the picture and the apology side by side.'

I don't manage to convince Máki that waiting is worthwhile. He agrees to let me have my way this time, but no more than twenty-four hours.

A message from Ludmilla tells me she's arriving tomorrow night.

I decide to put off piling pressure on Svanhvít until I've grilled Ludmilla. In a manner of speaking. I want to know not just about her role at New Baltic Models, but also everything about Ilona and Robertas and their links to the Baltic mafia.

Then Lísa Björk brings another nugget of negative news concerning the search for Ásthildur.

'Hjördís Eyjólfsdóttir's funeral took place in the Kópavogur church and I found the name of the priest who officiated, but unfortunately, he's dead,' she says.

Hell!

'Hjördís is buried in Fossvogur,' Lísa Björk continues. 'According to the churchyard records, it's a single grave.'

'Of course.'

'I can't find anything in the public system relating to a possible funeral for Ásthildur Ásvaldsdóttir.'

'Which is another indication that the entry in the national database stating that Ásthildur died in 1972, like her mother, is false,' I reply. 'It's a pack of bullshit and lies, courtesy of Hermann Rögnvaldsson.'

A new idea pops into my head.

'Did she get a new date of birth?'

Lísa Björk looks up from the screen of her little laptop with an enquiring look on her face.

'Ásthildur was born on the 25th of May 1971. Isn't it likely that the child could have held on to the same date of birth, despite getting new parents and a new name?'

'Could be.'

'See if you can get a list of all living Icelandic women born on the same day as Ásthildur. That could give us a few clues.'

'OK.'

I'm painfully aware that no progress is being made in the search for Ásthildur.

We've hit the brick walls of the system at every turn. These are the walls that ruthless men erected around their lies years ago.

Sheesh!

I open up the fireproof filing cabinet. I pick out the cigar box that Hákon handed to me on his death bed. Once again I examine the photograph of Hjördís Eyjólfsdóttir, busy painting the farmhouse at Hvítanes blue.

The envelope Hákon gave me to hand to his daughter is still in the box.

Any reason I shouldn't open it? Could it help in the search for her?

I withstand the temptation.

After thinking it over, I place the picture of Hjördís on the desk, above the computer keyboard. From there, this creased photo of a smiling girl up a ladder will be there in front of me. It'll stay there until I can fulfil the old man's dying wish.

Charity is the flickering light of a candle in the darkness of the soul, as Mother said.

32

Raggi keeps his word. He sends me copies of the police reports that relate in one way or another to Sverrir Guðbjartsson's numerous offences.

The city's finest have twice taken statements from his girlfriend at Bessastaðir.

During the second interview, they tried their damnedest to get Sveinfríður Tómasdóttir to admit that Sverrir had been awake when she got into the car.

But she sticks to her testimony. She didn't notice whether Sverrir was awake or asleep. That's because he was lying rather than sitting in the back, and wore dark glasses. So she hadn't been able to see his eyes.

According to Sveinfríður, she got behind the wheel and took the car out onto the Bessastaðir drive without saying a word to Sverrir. It wasn't until the car was past the roundabout and on out on the Álftanes road that anything was said.

This testimony maintains the possibility that Sverrir's telling the truth. That he really had been fast asleep on the back seat of the car while Benedikt Björgúlfsson was murdered within the walls built of the thick Gálgahraun rock.

I also read with interest the blackbirds' report of finding the candlesticks at Sverrir's place. In fact, it's surprising that it's so short.

According to the report, an unnamed informer told the

police that Sverrir had a substantial amount of narcotics in his room. Two blackbirds who were on duty downtown were sent to the location at around two in the morning. The door was unlocked and Sverrir was asleep in his bed. They tried to wake him, with little success. So they started to search for dope in his room. There was nothing of that nature to be found, but they stumbled instead across the candlesticks under the bed. As the coppers were certain that this was something Sverrir must have stolen, they took him and the stolen goods along to the station at Hlemmur. Further questioning was postponed until the suspect had slept it all off.

I put the document aside and think it over.

Who told the cops to look in Sverrir's room that night? In a place where no dope was found?

Suspicions pop up one after another.

Could this informer have known about the Bessastaðir murder weapon hidden under Sverrir's bed? Was that why this person had pointed the blackbirds in that direction?

It's certainly a possibility.

I pull the keyboard over, and send an email to Fat Raggi demanding to know the informer's identity.

There's not much to be had among all the other reports in the bundle. Some are just terse accounts of break-ins and thefts. These are the petty crimes that finance his drug habit, to which Sverrir Guðbjartsson has already admitted.

There's also nothing new in the testimony of the witnesses who were present at Bessastaðir when the body was found – and I'm one of them. Staff at the Presidential residence don't have anything substantive to add, other than that one confirms that the church had been unlocked on the day Benedikt Björgúlfsson was murdered. No key was needed to get into God's house.

I read through the account the city's finest have provided of the items found on the body.

Benedikt was wearing a pinstriped Armani suit. The keys

of his car were in the left jacket pocket. That's a Porsche 911. It was waiting for its late owner in the parking lot on the north side of Bessastaðir. There's also a pure white handkerchief of Chinese silk. Phone in the right pocket, a Nokia. Benedikt's driving licence was in the breast pocket, along with an American Express card. In the inside jacket pocket is a brownish card with Japanese or Chinese lettering. Could be an invitation, suggests the report's author.

A Japanese or Chinese invitation? Where from?

Again pulling the keyboard close, I send the cops a question about the mysterious foreign card that could be some kind of invitation.

Raggi gets back to me that afternoon.

'The drug squad's informer is confidential, for reasons of this person's safety,' he writes. 'There are only two people on the force who are in touch with this man and know his real name. I have no idea what his name is.'

But he's attached a picture of the invitation card that was found in Benedikt's pocket, as if that's some kind of consolation,

For a while I stare at the unintelligible characters on the screen. Then I hit the print button. I place the result on Lísa Björk's desk.

'Do you know anyone who understands this stuff?'

'Is it Chinese?' she asks.

'Or Japanese.'

'I know a Japanese girl who's studying geology at the university,' Lísa Björk says, reaching for the phone.

Back in my office, I immerse myself in a complex debt case that I'll have to represent in court in the coming weeks and months.

An hour or so later, Lísa Björk appears, with a little Japanese doll at her side.

'Mariko says it's definitely not an invitation.'

'What, then?'

The Japanese girl picks up the brown paper with its black lettering.

'These symbols are for the Japanese word *fukushuu*,' she says in English.

'Meaning what?'

'Vengeance.'

'Vengeance?'

'That's it,' Lísa Björk replies. 'These letters symbolise revenge.'

I lean back in my black boss man chair. I look at them in turn.

'A threat of revenge? In Japanese? In Benedikt Björgúlfsson's pocket?'

'Yes.'

'She's sure?'

'Oh, yes.'

'So Benedikt received a threatening letter in Japanese,' I muse. 'Presumably before he was murdered in the church. Although the murderer could have slipped that into his pocket afterwards.'

Lísa Björk nods.

'But it doesn't matter when Benedikt received this letter,' I say with a delighted smile. 'We'll call it a threatening letter and see if we can use it to blow holes in the case against my client.'

33

Saturday 17th January

The morning is bright but cold.

Despite the chill, a few thousand people have gathered around Jón Sigurðsson's statue on Austurvöllur. That's the nineteenth-century guy who was turned into a hero a few decades after his death. All the same, plenty of people loathed him during his lifetime.

Freyja Dögg has taken a stand right in front of the speaker's microphone. She's waving a placard with red lettering, demanding the government resign. Right now!

I can't be bothered to listen to the last speech all the way through. Instead, I hold my daughter's hand as we head over to Café Paris.

Sóley Árdís demands ice cream. I refresh myself with black coffee.

My mobile rings.

'What happened to Bjarni?' Máki asks – no greeting.

'Which lousy Bjarni?'

'Central Bank Bjarni Bjarnason, of course. You filed a lawsuit against him the other day for driving over some girl.'

'Yes, of course. What about him?'

'I heard he's dead.'

'Dead? How?'

'No idea,' Máki replies. 'I was hoping you'd heard something.'

'Nope. Nothing.'

'Maybe he was overcome by Benedikt's funeral.'

'Hmm.'

'But it's a hell of a coincidence, if Bjarni kicks the bucket the day after his old pal Bensi's buried, don't you think?'

'I don't believe in coincidences.'

'You don't?'

'No. Everything happens for a reason. Start to finish. That's the way nature works.'

Máki quickly says goodbye.

It goes without saying that I don't care a jot if the Central Bank guy is dead. His death doesn't affect me in the slightest. Except that the cops will subsequently sideline Freyja Dögg's lawsuit. Case dead and buried. Just like that man.

That's if he really is dead.

I call my fat cop friend to find out.

'I can't comment on that case,' Raggi snaps.

'Come on. I just want to know if the man is alive or dead.'

'There'll be a statement this afternoon.'

'Really?'

'That's all I have to say about this.'

'So he's dead?'

'If you say so.'

'So there has to be something out of the ordinary about this if there's a special press statement about this man's death. Am I right?'

'I'm answering no more questions.'

'I mean, you don't make a habit of issuing statements about normal fatalities?'

'Goodbye.'

Raggi hangs up.

I get a fresh cup of coffee, and call Máki. Line engaged. I get through on the third attempt.

'Know anything more?'

'Yep. The cops are all over Bjarni Bjarnason's summer

palace in Selfoss,' the old newshound replies. 'My sources tell me that a forensic team from Reykjavík arrived around midday and they're examining the garage that adjoins the house.'

'Which means suspected what? Suicide?'

'Or murder.'

'Hardly.'

'It's possible.'

'I gather the cops are issuing a statement later today. But you didn't hear that from me.'

'Not a word.'

Protestors are still surging away from Austurvöllur when I clip Sóley Árdís back into the silver steed. I head home.

The first report of Bjarni Bjarnason's death appears on *News Blog* that afternoon.

Found dead in his garage

Bjarni Bjarnason, a longstanding senior figure at the Central Bank, was found deceased in the garage adjoining his summer home in Selfoss shortly before midday today. Police are investigating the circumstances of his death, and no other information has been made available.

Máki pads the article out with a lot of stuff about the deceased's long career. He was divorced. Two grown-up daughters. At the end he adds:

Bjarni Bjarnason was one of the pallbearers at the funeral of his friend Benedikt Björgúlfsson, which took place in the Reykjavík cathedral only yesterday. As has already been reported, Benedikt was murdered in the church at Bessastaðir two weeks ago.

Máki neatly links the two. That'll shake up the city's finest.

Freyja Dögg calls just after six.

'The cops were here earlier,' she says, sounding upset.

'They wanted to know what I was up to yesterday evening and during the night.'

'Really?'

'But they wouldn't tell me why they wanted to ask all these horrible intrusive questions, so I told them you're my lawyer and they can talk to you.'

'Good for you. So where were you?'

'We were preparing for the protest well into the night.'

'And you have plenty of witnesses?'

Freyja Dögg views the question as an odd one.

'You're making it sound like I need an alibi.'

'It wouldn't do any harm.'

'Why?'

'Bjarni Bjarnason's dead.'

'What did you say? Dead?'

'Let me know if they come back,' I continue. 'I need to be present for any interrogation, if it comes to that.'

Freyja Dögg doesn't reply right away.

'Hell,' she says after a long pause. 'Now my mother's going to go properly nuts.'

34

Saturday night, 17th January

I wait restlessly for Ludmilla.

Her evening flight from Copenhagen landed at Keflavík airport. Right now she's driving her rental car along Reykjanesbraut, into the city.

I wander from room to room of the upper floor. It's a circuit – living room, kitchen, and the bedroom where Sóley Árdís is fast asleep.

There are conflicting emotions fighting it out in my heart.

Love and shock.

Suspicion.

All the same, I'm down the stairs in a flash when the doorbell rings. All I'm wearing is a silk robe. I hold Ludmilla tight there in the hallway. All my doubts are forgotten.

For the moment.

She places a bottle of Jack D on the kitchen table. She pours while I wait for the Nespresso machine to fill two cups.

The Tennessee nectar meets the ink-black espresso. It's a marriage made in heaven.

But duty calls.

We both know that this moment of truth can't wait.

'Dagnija is OK,' Ludmilla says.

'She called. Ilona is still being held.'

'What do you mean, held?'

'She's being held as a hostage of some kind,' I reply.

'Hostage? What for?'

'So that Robertas doesn't blab.'

Ludmilla hears out my theory that the criminals Robertas is involved with have kidnapped Ilona and are holding her as a way of ensuring he doesn't tell the boys in black anything.

'It could be,' she says. 'I'm not in that business.'

'No?'

'No. I'm working only with New Baltic Models. That's my business now.'

She explains how she came to own the agency. It was part of her father's business empire back when she first came to Iceland to dance for El Dorado's customers. That was years ago.

'I so rarely met my father because he travelled all the time. But three years ago he turned up unannounced in Riga and told me that New Baltic Models was all mine. He said that was his legacy to me.'

'I see.'

'I now have hundreds of girls on the books. These are girls who want more money, and they know there's money to be made in the west. They come to me from Russia and Lithuania and Hungary, from Romania and Bulgaria. New Baltic Models is my only business and I make sure it stays legal, no smuggling or anything else.'

'But you know who sent Robertas to Iceland with some drugs?'

'I asked Sergei about this,' Ludmilla says. 'He said that when Dad was seriously ill, there was a power struggle for his business. Dad wanted Sergei to take over the whole thing, but there were others who didn't like that idea, and now there are two groups trying to get control.'

'I see.'

'Sergei says Robertas isn't one of his guys, and I believe that.'

'So whose is he?'

'He says he has a competitor who wants to take over all the business in Iceland.'

'Take over what? The drug scene?'

Ludmilla nods.

'I only know what Sergei has told me, but I know he's telling me the truth. He's protected me for a long time and I always trust him.'

'Did you know that Robertas and Ilona are a couple?'

She shakes her head.

'I don't get to know my girls at a personal level. Just business,' she replies. 'I didn't know anything about this Robertas until you mentioned him. But Sergei knew right away who he is.'

'So Sergei must know who Robertas meant to meet in Iceland?'

Ludmilla nods.

'Do you know?'

'No. But Sergei gave me the name of the place where they process the gear. It's some old farm.'

'They have a drug lab in a farmhouse here in Iceland?'

'Yep.'

'And you know the name of the farm?'

'Yes.'

Finally, at last. Good news.

'That's where these bastards could be holding Ilona.'

'I don't know. But Sergei says these are dangerous men.'

I can see she's troubled.

'Of course I wouldn't dream of heading off there on my own like some kind of superhero,' I say with a smile. 'I'll have to find a way to get the drug squad to raid the place.'

Ludmilla doesn't return my smile.

'Sergei says that the police in Iceland are like a burst pipe.'

'A burst pipe?'

'You know. Like a pipe that leaks and leaks.'

'Aha.'

I empty my glass.

'We ought to make plans when it's daylight,' I say, getting to my feet.

She nods.

Ludmilla is some time preparing for the night.

I wait impatiently in the bedroom, naked beneath the warm duvet.

She's wearing only a short, transparent silk nightdress. She stands in the doorway, hands on her hips. There's a provocative look on her face.

I lift the duvet, and see the flicker of desire in her dark eyes.

Ludmilla takes slow steps over to the bed. She straddles me nimbly, leans forward. There's hunger in her kisses.

'I'm going to love you all night long,' she says breathlessly.

I raise my hands to the neckline of her nightdress.

'Yes!' she gasps as I rip it open. 'Yes!'

Early in the morning I wake next to Ludmilla, who's sleeping soundly.

I sit up in bed. Cautiously, I move the duvet aside.

For a long time I admire her naked form. Powerful legs. Pert nipples. Delicious lips.

Eventually, I have to admit to myself that my feelings have changed.

What was supposed to be love that would last a lifetime has gone from my heart.

That's the ice-cold reality.

All the same, there's no point being miserable.

Lust lives on, even when love dies, as Mother said.

35

Sunday 18th January

I don't trust anyone.

Not even Ludmilla. She's too trusting of Sergei, her protector.

The morning's spent gathering information about the place the dope dealers from Lithuania are using.

Efstakot is at the top of Borgarfjörður. It's not far from the Húsafell summer house district. That's where Icelandic families go to find their carefully organised rural paradise.

The registered owner of the farmland, which for a long time was state property, is in fact called Paradise. It's a limited company that over the last few years appears to have amassed something of a portfolio of former state-owned land.

But Paradise is wholly owned by a property company in Luxembourg.

A few phone calls are all that's needed to establish that the Luxembourg company is owned by Gunnar Kjartan and Benedikt Björgúlfsson.

Intriguing.

According to publicly available documents, Aðalsteinn Oddsson has a horse breeding enterprise at Efstakot. But there's no other agricultural activity there, no indication of habitation.

Aðalsteinn Oddsson?

I've a feeling the name's somehow familiar. Time to look through the national register.

There are three living Aðalsteinns who are also Oddsson. One of them's married to Oddný Vestmann. That's Gunnar Kjartan's sister.

Senior police officer Aðalsteinn Oddsson.

Aha!

This has to be the one Rósalind said has authority over the police college. He's Glúmur's old man, the copper who fetched Ilona from El Dorado on 27th December.

The pieces are starting to fit together to form a clearer picture.

It's not a pretty picture. Robertas, Ilona and Glúmur, dope on an industrial scale, Aðalsteinn and Efstakot.

All the same, I'm struggling to cope with the idea of a senior blackbird being involved with drug production at Efstakot.

But Glúmur? That shitbag could be capable of anything.

The connections linking Efstakot with Aðalsteinn and Glúmur are deeply worrying.

How am I supposed to convince the cops that there's a drug factory run on a farm where Aðalsteinn Oddsson breeds horses? One of their own people?

While I give Sóley Árdís her breakfast, I think things over.

After a long discussion, Ludmilla agrees with my gut feeling that Svanhvít is the key. The best way to get Gunnbjörn Hannesson to do the right thing is to break her down. She has to admit to her role as a go-between for the Lithuanian mafiosi, and put the guardians of law and order onto the gang's factory at Efstakot.

I go through the options, and write a long list of everything that needs to be done.

Then it's getting to work systematically.

The first call is to my cousin Sissi. My personal technical genius takes three hours to take all the necessary measures.

Then a call to Svanhvít.

She's happy to meet that afternoon. I tell her we're meeting Robertas.

Gunnbjörn is a challenge. The drug squad supremo has suspected me of being two-faced from the word go. But he finally agrees to listen to my plans.

When everything's ready, I leave my little darling in Lísa Björk's care. She also needs to take care of Gunnbjörn and the office. I'm collecting Svanhvít myself.

She lives in one of the new houses in the Vellir district. It's a stone's throw from the vast Alcoa aluminium smelter at Straumsvík.

Svanhvít sits in the passenger seat, as quiet as a mouse. She stares silently at the road ahead. Then I turn the silver steed onto Reykjanesbraut and head west.

'Aren't we going out east to Litla-Hraun?' she asks.

'First you need to take a lie detector test,' I say, and put my foot down.

She's startled.

'What do you mean?'

'Robertas told me the whole story.'

'What story?'

'That the gang he was working for have kidnapped his girlfriend.'

'What girlfriend?'

'They're holding Ilona to ensure his loyalty, and his silence.'

'Who is Ilona?' Svanhvít asks.

Her voice shakes.

'And that you have been systematically passing on messages from the gang.'

'Me?'

'That means that you're as guilty of deprivation of liberty as the kidnappers themselves.'

'I've never heard anything so ridiculous,' Svanhvít replies, but she doesn't manage to summon a laugh.

'I can prove that you passed messages to Robertas from

the kidnappers,' I continue. 'I recorded our last conversation.'

'You're lying.'

I'm driving fast, one hand on the wheel. With the other hand I get the little recorder from the glove compartment. I play her part of the conversation at Litla-Hraun.

I switch it off after a minute, and drop it into my pocket.

'You don't understand a word of Lithuanian,' she protests feebly.

'You're not the only translator out there.'

'Oh.'

'I can prove that you've been working for a foreign crime organisation. That you've misled the Icelandic authorities and hindered investigations. But first of all there'll be many years behind bars for kidnap and false imprisonment.'

Svanhvít cracks up, and dissolves into tears.

'You only have one option open to you,' I continue. 'And that's to tell me the truth, the whole truth and nothing but the truth.'

'I didn't kidnap anyone.'

'Tell me right now who took Ilona.'

'I just know that two men from Lithuania are looking after her,' Svanhvít snivels.

'Where?'

'In the countryside.'

'Where in the countryside?'

'They're on a farm in Borgarfjörður. I think it's called Efstibær or Efstakot, or something like that.'

'Have you seen her there?'

'No. I've never been there.'

'Who told you she's at Efstakot?'

Svanhvít bursts into tears again.

'You'll have to tell me everything if you want me to help you.'

'It was Glúmur,' she mutters.

'Glúmur Aðalsteinsson?'

'Yes.'

'And the messages you took to Robertas? Were they from Glúmur?'

She nods.

'Answer me.'

'Yes, he forced me to.'

'Forced you to? What does he have on you?'

'I don't want to say.'

'Why?'

Svanhvít takes off her glasses. She wipes her eyes with a white handkerchief.

'It's nothing to do with this matter,' she finally replies.

'All right. We'll leave that for the moment.'

In half an hour I'm outside the red townhouse. I push Svanhvít ahead of me and into the meeting room where Gunnbjörn Hannesson and Lísa Björk are waiting.

Svanhvít looks at the drug squad chief with terror in her eyes.

'Sit,' I say.

There's a screen on the table that's still displaying the silver steed's passenger seat.

'We heard the whole conversation,' Lísa Björk says.

'You're in the shit up to your neck, darling,' Gunnbjörn says, his voice ice-cold. 'I presume you're going to be co-operative and won't conceal anything important.'

Svanhvít falls forward onto the desk, crying her eyes out.

36

The drug squad's top dog isn't easily convinced.

To be honest, he was totally in denial to start with. He absolutely refused to believe that Aðalsteinn Oddsson or his son could be in cahoots with Lithuanian criminals.

'I've known Aðalsteinn for years,' he grated. 'He's as honest as the day is long.'

'It's quite a few days since I received evidence linking Glúmur to Ilona's disappearance,' I replied. I showed him the screengrab of the two young boys in black with the Latvian girl between them. They're next to Glúmur's jeep, outside Porno Valdi's strip joint.

All the same, the drug squad chief does his best to tie Svanhvít in knots. He's hoping to trash the plausibility of her account. But he doesn't get her to change her story.

Svanhvít is certainly a nervous wreck at this point. But she also seems relieved. It's as if shackles have been removed from her now that she can tell the truth.

'There's no doubt about Glúmur's links to the Lithuanian mafiosi,' I say finally. 'You'll just have to accept the reality of there being black sheep in the police, just as everywhere else in society. And you need to take immediate action.'

Gunnbjörn looks at me questioningly.

'Action? What action?'

'Ilona needs to be freed as soon as possible. The best option is a raid on the drugs factory at Efstakot under cover of darkness.'

He mulls it over.

'First I need to interrogate Robertas to get Svanhvít's story confirmed.'

'In that case I'll hold you personally responsible for whatever happens to Ilona.'

'How so?'

'I consider that Ilona is in great danger,' I reply. 'Every minute that passes without direct action increases the likelihood that Glúmur will get wind of Svanhvít's confession. He'll undoubtedly take desperate measures to protect himself.'

'Desperate measures?' Gunnbjörn repeats.

'Yes. Glúmur acts first and thinks afterwards. He capable of anything.'

The drug squad supremo gets to his feet. He paces back and forth in deep thought.

'I'll need a warrant,' he says at last.

'Remember that the fewer people who are aware of this confession, the better Ilona's chances are.'

He halts next to Svanhvít.

'You'll need to sign a statement,' he says.

She nods.

'Then you'll have to confirm it before a judge.'

'Yes.'

'Come on, then.'

Gunnbjörn takes Svanhvít's arm firmly. He leads her out to an unmarked police car that's parked in front of the red town house.

The city's finest confirm on the evening news that Bjarni Bjarnason's death is being treated as murder.

They refuse to provide any further information about how the murder took place. They make it clear that there's no suspect in the picture.

'I know why the cops are walking on eggshells around this,' Máki says.

'Let's hear it.'

'The main reason is Gunnar Kjartan Vestmann.'

'In what way?'

'On Friday afternoon, after Bensi's funeral, Bjarni, Gunnar Kjartan and the Reverend Hildibrandur all went out east to Selfoss and held their own wake for their departed comrade. From what I've heard, they stayed drinking well into the night.'

'You don't imagine that they might have done their pal in?'

'No. I'm just making the point that nobody knows yet how Bjarni was murdered that night after his friends had gone home.'

'Who found him?'

'I understand that Bjarni's daughter had been trying to call him. He wasn't picking up so she asked a friend living in Selfoss to drop in on him around midday. The friend found all the doors were shut and nobody came to the door when she rang the bell, but she could see through the garage window that his jeep was in there. So Bjarni's daughter called the police and asked them to check on the place, and they found the body in the garage.'

'How was he killed?'

'Nobody wants to say. But I'll keep digging.'

I call Gunnbjörn around nine that evening to find out what's happening.

'All clear to go,' he says cautiously.

'So when's it happening?'

'Around midnight.'

'I'm coming with you.'

'That's out of the question.'

'I need to look after Ilona when you find her.'

'Our people are perfectly capable of that.'

'She's my baby.'

It takes a while for the drug squad chief to give way.

He doesn't give in until I've convinced him that I'll be there anyway. I'll make my own way if I'm not going to be with them.

'But you have to wait in a car until the building has been secured,' he says. 'Anything else is not acceptable.'

'Safety is paramount?' I say with a laugh.

'I'll send a car to fetch you at midnight. On the dot.'

He hangs up.

Lísa Björk isn't impressed with this decision of mine.

'Didn't Ludmilla say that these men are very dangerous?' she asks, worried.

'I can be dangerous as well if I put my mind to it,' I reply, and go to dig out some suitable clothes for night-time action.

37

Monday 19th January, early hours

There's a wind blowing off the icecaps of Eiríksjökull and Langjökull that's as cold as hell. It whistles westwards down the valley. It sets up a morose whine in the branches of the copse where the drug squad chief's fleet of cars is out of sight of prying eyes.

A waxing moon wades through the clouds. It hides behind the dark banks of cumulus. Occasionally it breaks through and bathes the valley in ghostly light.

The buildings of Efstakot huddle beneath a steep hillside. These are dark outlines that show up every time the moon lights up the night.

The farmhouse is two storeys. The outbuildings are around fifty metres away. There's a newish stable and a yard, as well as a dilapidated old cowshed.

An outdoor light burns in the yard, not far from the farmhouse door. There's another light by the entrance to the outbuilding.

The fleet departed from the police headquarters in Reykjavík around one in the morning. Two squad cars and a minibus.

The chief ushers me into one of the squad cars. There are two women already sitting there. Both of them say they have many years of drug squad experience behind them.

The fleet went in convoy through the Hvalfjörður tunnel

and up to Reykholt, where Snorri Sturluson was done to death 800 years ago. He was a greedy old guy who spent his evenings writing stories.

'Fifteen minutes between vehicles,' Gunnbjörn Hannesson says over the comms system. He headed off first in the other car.

We were at the back of the convoy, behind the minibus.

The driver knew exactly where the other vehicles had parked out of sight. He drove the last few kilometres with no lights so as not to give us away.

There's probably no need, as it looks like the criminals at Efstakot are fast asleep.

Gunnbjörn prepares his men for action. There are black-clad Special Unit guys together with others from the drug squad. Ten men, two women, one sniffer dog.

They're well equipped. The night-vision gear on their heads is reminiscent of a rhinoceros horn.

'I need to see in the dark as well,' I say.

'No,' he repeats. 'You're staying here.'

The group vanish into the woods.

I tug the zip of my black coverall up to my neck, and pull my hat down to my ears. I'm waiting for the moon to show me the way.

Finally, I'm able to hurry along behind them.

In some places they clamber over barbed wire fences that have fallen into the grass. They make quick progress up the pasture towards the buildings. They're stooped forward like old men.

I follow fast behind them. Feeling my way past the worst of the patches of ice.

The winter cold has lasted for so long that the pasture is slippery underfoot.

The blackbirds divide into two teams. Two of the armed Special Unit officers take their positions by the back door of the farmhouse. Two more pad over to the stable. The others wait in the yard.

On Gunnbjörn's signal, the boys in black make their move.

The front door gives way as a sledgehammer smashes it in. Lights go on in the hallway. They storm into the building, one after another.

In an astonishingly short time, there are lights in every room, upstairs and down.

I go into the hallway.

Some of the Special Unit guys come down the stairs with two men in handcuffs. They've clearly just woken up, and have no idea what's hit them.

Gunnbjörn goes ahead of them to the living room on the ground floor, a lounge with a new sofa and a large flatscreen TV. The two men are made to sit on the leather sofa. Standing in front of them, he delivers a barrage of questions in Icelandic, and then in English.

He gets no answers. The pair of prisoners, who look to be in their thirties, shake their heads. They pretend they don't understand. Then they stare gloomily at the floor.

Gunnbjörn has finally had enough.

'Keep them here,' he tells two of his officers.

The chief splits his team again. Some are sent to search the farmhouse and others to check the outbuildings.

'Let's have the sniffer dog go through the house first,' he says.

I hang around in the living room. I look the prisoners up and down.

'Where's Ilona?' I ask in English.

They look up smartly.

The question clearly takes them by surprise.

'You must be aware that kidnap is a much more serious crime than peddling dope,' I continue. 'You're going to be locked up for a long time.'

'I don't think you're supposed to talk to them,' one of the blackbirds warns.

'Do yourselves a favour,' I say. 'Tell me where Ilona is.'

But they just look down at their bare feet.

Gunnbjörn stamps down the stairs.

'The girl isn't here,' he says.

'And the outbuildings?'

'They're still searching,' he replies.

I go out into the hall, and up the stairs.

There are two bedrooms. Two sofa beds in one, and there's a double bed in the other. All the beds are made up.

The dog sniffs the bedclothes on the double bed.

'Were those guys asleep?' I ask.

'Yep, nabbed them both in bed,' the blackbird replies.

'Here?'

'No. In the smaller bedroom.'

He carefully watching the dog's reactions as it sniffs around the wardrobe.

'So who slept here?' I ask.

The cop shrugs.

I sit on the bed, and watch the dog at work for a while.

'He's only looking for drugs, isn't he?'

'Yes. That's what he's trained for.'

Once the blackbird has led the dog back down the stairs, I get to my feet. I peer into the open wardrobe.

Some of the shelves are empty. On others are underwear, socks, shirts and sweater that badly need a visit to a washing machine. The same goes for the towels and the filthy bedclothes.

Typical male housekeeping.

I find no female clothes. Nothing indicates that Ilona could have been held in this room for weeks on end.

Gunnbjörn clatters up the stairs.

'We've found the factory,' he says cheerfully.

'But not Ilona?'

He shakes his head.

'She must be here,' I say.

'Where, then?'

I follow the chief down the stairs to the living room.

'Put them in the car,' he says.

'You're going back to town right away?'

'Some of the team will stay here to gather evidence, but I'm taking these two back to town to question them with the help of a good translator,' Gunnbjörn says.

I snatch at one prisoner's shoulder, and look into his dark eyes.

'Where is Ilona?'

A smirk passes over his lips.

'Where is she?' I demand.

The man looks away.

'Enough. Get them out of here,' Gunnbjörn orders. 'You're coming as well.'

'No,' I reply. 'Not until I've found Ilona.'

38

No way am I giving up.

I'm convinced that Ilona is somewhere here at Efstakot – alive or dead.

That cunning smirk on the face of one of those arrested proves it.

But where?

The drug squad team are still gathering evidence in the old cowshed. That's where they found a few litres of amphetamine base, and all the gear needed to turn it into saleable tablets.

They refuse to let me inside, so as not to compromise the investigation.

'We've searched high and low in this building,' a young blackbird says, blocking the doorway. 'The woman isn't here. That's for sure.'

I head back out into the darkness of the night. I make cautiously for the stable. It's a fairly new timber building. The walls are clad in reddish corrugated steel sheets.

There are ten stalls for horses. Six are empty. I stroke the occupants of the remaining four, who nuzzle me as if I'm a welcome visitor. At the same time, I search through each stall in turn. No luck.

In the neighbouring barn bundles of hay are piled high. But there's no obvious hiding place any more than in the stable itself.

Hell!

I walk gloomily back to the white-walled farmhouse. Lights burn in every room.

I'm fully aware that the boys in black searched the farmhouse from top to bottom without finding any sign of Ilona. But they could have missed something.

I shift all of the furniture in the living room. Tap on the walls. Open every cupboard and sideboard. This is all in the desperate hope that there's a hiding place big enough for a person, alive or dead.

But the results are the same. There's nobody in the living room.

A black cat jumps onto the table in the kitchen, and licks the unwashed plates.

It looks up as I come in. Its yellow eyes challenge me as it stares. As I approach, it hisses. Then it jumps off the table and runs out of the room.

It's a pigsty!

Didn't these wankers ever learn to wash up?

A small washroom leads off the kitchen. It seems to be used as a pantry. In any case, there's plenty of cases of beer and soft drinks, and a freezer that's stacked with pizza boxes.

There's a light on the washing machine, although its cycle finished a long time ago.

I switch it off, open the door and pull out the damp clothes.

There are a few shirts – and some flimsy underwear. Clearly feminine.

Bingo!

Ilona has been here. No doubt about it.

The question is whether she's still here at Efstakot – and where?

I know she's not in any of the outbuildings. She's not down here on the ground floor. There's no sign that there's a cellar under the building.

The only hope is that she's somewhere on the upper floor.

I start searching the cramped bathroom. There's just space for a shower and a toilet.

Next I go carefully through the bedroom where the two men were nabbed. There's nothing to be found under the beds but clothes of theirs, at varying levels of filthy.

Finally I try the main bedroom. This is where I've already searched.

The black cat has made itself comfortable next to the bed, tight against the drawer for bedclothes. It seems to extend all the way under the bed.

It glares at me with its yellow eyes. But it doesn't move.

I look around, and open the wardrobe again, to make certain.

Fucking hell!

The cat's watching my every movement. It hisses when I approach the bed.

There's no hiding place here.

Or is there?'

'Get away with you!' I yell, and wave my right hand.

Once the black cat's jumped onto the bed, I catch hold of the drawer and haul it out onto the floor.

A large black sheet has been placed over the drawer's contents. I snatch it away and there's Ilona.

The girl's pale. No make-up. Her eyes are shut.

She's also tied hand and foot.

I put a hand to her neck. I feel the warmth, and a pulse.

She's alive.

I clatter down the stairs, and run out to the cowshed, yelling at the boys in black who come running.

They untie her and lift her onto the bed.

One of them brings a first aid kit. He listens to the girl's heartbeat and measures her heart rate. He shines a little torch into her eyes.

'I reckon they must have given her a heavy dose of dope, or sleeping pills,' he says. 'Her heart rate's more or less normal for someone in a deep sleep.'

'We need to get her to hospital right away,' I say.

The blackbird calls Gunnbjörn. He's already in Reykjavík.

'He's getting an ambulance from Akranes sent out to us,' the boy in black says. 'It'll be here in an hour or so.'

I sit on the bed at the girl's side. I hold her hand for a while.

Then I fish the mobile phone from my pocket and call Dagnija.

She's wide awake the moment I give her the good news she's been waiting such a long time for, that her friend has been found.

'Thank God!' she squawks.

I don't bother mentioning to her that there's no sign that mythical old geezer has ever shown his face at Efstakot.

39

Monday 19th January

Ilona's at the National Hospital. She's unconscious.

I don't leave for home until the drug squad's top dog has agreed to keep one of his men at the hospital. The Latvian girl's safety has to be ensured, at least until she comes round from her drugged stupor.

The doctors expect her to wake around midday.

Máki's waiting for me in the lobby of the hospital.

The veteran newshound is getting progressively greyer.

Apart from that, he hasn't changed a lot. He's as skinny as always. It's as if he doesn't give himself time to eat properly. He's still wearing the same shabby leather jacket as always.

'Is the girl all right?' he says, straight to the point.

'We'll find out when she comes around.'

I give Máki a quick run-down of the operation at Efstakot. I see no reason not to mention that I was the one who found Ilona, not the city's finest.

Finally, I encourage Máki to look into the farm's ownership, and into who has been renting the place for the last few years.

'Won't you just tell me?' he asks.

'It's better if you find it out for yourself.'

I point him towards Gunnbjörn Hannesson who'll supply information about the drugs that were found in the old cowshed, and about the two Lithuanian crims.

Ilona's my concern, not the drugs business at Efstakot.

'I took Sóley Árdís to nursery,' Lísa Björk tells me when I finally get back to the red town house around ten that morning.

I start with a shower, before starting at the office. I'm hoping the pounding flow of water will cleanse body and soul.

Right away, I'm feeling better.

At midday there's a message from the National Hospital. Ilona's conscious.

When I march into her room at around two o'clock, she has no idea who I am.

That's understandable.

Ilona doesn't want to talk to me. But that changes when I give her Dagnija on the other end of the phone. For quite a while I sit as she talks to her old friend in their own language, of which I don't understand a word.

The joy in Ilona's eyes tells me everything I need to know.

Gunnbjörn arrives shortly afterwards, bringing two sidekicks with him – and Haraldur Haraldsson, the stuck-up chief who refused to authorise a search for Ilona.

'What's this shitbag doing here?' I ask coldly.

'Ilona's disappearance was one of his cases,' Gunnbjörn replies. 'He needs to be present for the interview to sign the case off.'

'Haraldur's role was mainly to prevent any search being carried out.'

'At this point we only need to ask Ilona a few questions,' the chief continues, without replying directly. 'We'll dig deeper into the events of the last few weeks when she's been discharged from hospital.'

Nevertheless, the interview takes a good while. The interpreter has to translate Gunnbjörn's questions into Latvian, and Ilona's replies into Icelandic.

She's reluctant to say much about her treatment at Efstakot. But she confirms that Glúmur picked her up from El Dorado on the 27th. He also drove her out into the countryside after her strip routine for the police college.

'Sigvaldi said I could trust him, because they are good friends,' Ilona said.

Glúmur had offered a hefty bonus to entertain his friends at Efstakot. But once they were there, he ordered her to stay put for a few days. He took her phone off her, and left her with the two Lithuanian guys.

'Glúmur said he'd be back in two days, and then he didn't return.'

To begin with, the Lithuanians just locked Ilona in overnight.

'Then they forgot to lock the door and I sneaked out and down to the road,' she says. 'But there was no traffic, so they caught me and after that I was tied up and given an injection.'

After that escape attempt, Ilona was given an injection every night.

'I tried to get away again, and after that they started shutting me in that box before they went to sleep,' she says. 'After that I never woke up until after midday.'

Ilona immediately identifies the two Lithuanians when Gunnbjörn shows her pictures. And she fingers Glúmur.

'Yeah. That's the bastard who took me out into the countryside and left me there.'

'Thank you,' the drug squad supremo says finally, getting to his feet. 'That'll do for the moment.'

'I assume you've already arrested Glúmur,' I say.

'He'll be questioned shortly,' Gunnbjörn replies.

I stare at them both, Haraldur and the drug squad chief.

'Glúmur is still free?' I ask in astonishment.

'He has his rights, like anyone else,' Haraldur says.

'Rights? You mean the freedom to destroy evidence and threaten witnesses?'

'What witnesses?'

'Ilona, for instance. She's both a victim and a witness.'

'She's out of any danger.'

'Is Glúmur still on duty? Wearing the same uniform as you?'

'He's not on day shifts this week.'

'You're beyond hopeless.'

I turn my back on Haraldur.

'Will Ilona have continued protection here at the hospital?' I ask Gunnbjörn.

'That's not my decision,' the chief replies.

'Do I need to bring in a private bodyguard to ensure her safety? To protect her from Glúmur and his pals?'

'A police officer will be on duty here tonight,' Haraldur says. 'After that it's up to the Commissioner to decide.'

I stay for a while with Ilona after they've gone. I assure her she's in safe hands.

Then I talk to a doctor who expects Ilona will be ready to be discharged within twenty-four hours.

Máki's really gone to town on *News Blog*.

Not only is there a detailed account of Ilona's rescue, but also the photographs taken outside El Dorado. There are Glúmur and his pal Eiríkur – with Ilona between them. He's also written a sharply-worded article outlining Aðalsteinn Oddsson's links with Efstakot, where Ilona has been a prisoner for three weeks.

'Could these links explain the reluctance of the Reykjavík police to investigate Ilona's disappearance?' Máki asks. He portrays the Reykjavík Police Commissioner as not being competent to investigate this serious case, considering a number of his officers are implicated in it, in one way or another.

What Máki has to say is everywhere. All over social media, everywhere.

His words also alert the TV newshounds. They demand

an interview with Ilona. She flatly refuses to discuss her unpleasant experience with the media.

That evening I watch both stations' coverage, the interviews with me and Gunnbjörn concerning the search for Ilona, and the trove of drugs found at Efstakot. Then there are also Máki's allegations on *News Blog*.

'More than two weeks ago I demanded that the police initiate a search for Ilona,' I said in the interviews. 'Now we know that Ilona was in the hands of kidnappers at Efstakot. Last week I handed over solid evidence that two police officers had picked her up at El Dorado on the evening of 27th December. Their only response was to brand me a liar in a public statement, and to haul me up before the Bar Council's ethics committee! Of course it was a dereliction of duty on their part to not initiate an immediate search. In my opinion it is also worth asking whether police officers who have already been named in the media could have used their influence to prevent a search for Ilona from taking place.'

'Are there grounds for a public inquiry into the police's handling of this case?' the hack asks.

'At the very least, it calls for something more radical and transparent that the usual establishment cover-up, that's nothing more than a cat wash.'

'What do you mean by a cat wash?' Ludmilla asks.

'You know, like a cat licking itself clean.'

Once the newsreader has moved on to the state of fish stocks in Icelandic waters, I lean back on the sofa. My sweet little girl is in my arms.

'When Sóley Árdís is asleep, I can show you just how a cat licks,' I add with a smile.

40

Tuesday 20th January

Lísa Björk and I spend the entire morning going through the footage from Bessastaðir. That's the sequences from the CCTV that the Presidential security system recorded on old video tapes the day Benedikt Björgúlfsson met his killer in the church.

My only interest is sequences recorded between 1600 and 1800 on that day. At that time my client claims to have been asleep in his girlfriend's car in the parking lot not far from Bessastaðir. But I find no indication of any movement around the church. Nor is there any sign of Sveinfríður's car.

The city's finest say that one of the cameras at Bessastaðir was out of action that day. That happens to be precisely the one that should have been keeping an eye on God's house.

They claim to still be investigating how this could have happened.

'Can you give me an assurance that this tape hasn't simply been stolen?' I ask Raggi at lunchtime. The fat cop is in charge of the murder investigation at Bessastaðir.

'No,' he mutters grumpily. 'Unfortunately, we have no images from that camera, and no explanation as to why.'

'Did someone switch it off?'

'That's a possibility we're checking out.'

Hmmm.

'Doesn't this indicate that the murder had been planned in advance?'

'Not necessarily the murder.'

'Meaning what?'

'I consider that Benedikt was simply in the wrong place at the wrong time,' Raggi replies. 'On the other hand, it seems likely that the theft might have been prepared in advance, such as by switching off the security camera.'

'Who might have done that?'

'That's being investigated.'

'You don't suspect Sveinfríður or Sverrir of planning to rob the church?'

'We're checking every possibility.'

'That the girl could have switched off the camera?'

'We're ruling nothing out. That's all I have to say about this right now. I'm sure you understand, my dear Stella.'

Most of the footage shows guests dressed in their best arriving at Bessastaðir and departing later out into the winter cold. These are apparatchiks, politicians, money people, pillars of the cultural establishment.

It's like a cross-section of Iceland's power clique.

Only two of the guests are a surprise to me. That's not least because they appear to have come together.

I freeze the replay on the big screen in the meeting room.

Jónsteinn Ingólfsson, Porno Valdi's entertainments manager. And Glúmur Aðalsteinsson.

What are scum like this doing at a presidential reception at Bessastaðir?

I'm on the phone. I want to know from the President's office just why these two arsewipes were invited to the home of the leader of the nation for afternoon drinks. I badger one of the President's staff until I get what I want.

'We invited representatives of companies doing significant business with Germany to meet the new German ambassador,' the functionary replies. 'The two gentlemen you mention were there on behalf of *Icelandic Hotdrinks*, which imports large amounts of alcoholic beverages from Germany and also sells Icelandic liquor overseas.'

According to the company database, both Jónsteinn and Glúmur are on the board of this drinks company. So are Gunnar Kjartan Vestmann and Benedikt Björgúlfsson.

What a gang.

I call Máki.

'Gunnar Kjartan has fingers in pies everywhere, but he keeps it low-key,' he says. 'I've lost count of the companies he's bought or set up, either by himself or with one of his main clients. I couldn't tell you how many politicians whose paths to power he has supported financially. He's long been the most influential octopus in the Icelandic money clique.'

'And Jónsteinn? Or Glúmur?'

'I understand that Gunnar Kjartan has always had a soft spot for his nephew, as he has no children of his own,' Máki replies. 'And it's common knowledge that Jónsteinn has been one of his fixers for a long time.'

'I thought Jónsteinn was looking after Porno Valdi's affairs?'

'Good grief. Who do you think has Sigvaldi's back at El Dorado? Gunnar Kjartan may keep out of sight when it comes to any dirty business, but I hear it's his money that got Sigvaldi on his feet to start with.'

'So he's a typical paymaster?'

'That's it.'

I shudder.

'I hadn't figured out the connection,' I continue after a pause. 'But now I see the same thing wherever I look. Gunnar Kjartan was a close friend and business partner of Benedikt Björgúlfsson's, and Bjarni Bjarnason's, and they've both been murdered. He owns that dope den in Borgarfjörður that his brother-in-law rents. And his nephew kidnapped Ilona. It makes you wonder.'

'Yep. Gunnar Kjartan's hooks are into things everywhere.'

'Plus he was at Bessastaðir when Benedikt was murdered. Then he was drinking with his pals in Selfoss where Bjarni came to grief a few hours later.'

Máki is clearly unimpressed with this train of thought on my part. At any rate, he sees fit to warn me off.

'Tread very carefully if you're thinking of accusing Gunnar Kjartan of anything,' the old newshound says. 'He's a tough opponent, and he has a knack of deflecting blame onto others when things look bad.'

'I just feel it's repugnant.'

'Speaking of Bjarni, have you seen the latest on *News Blog*?'

'No.'

I call it up on the screen. The headline stares me in the face.

Murder by Land Cruiser

'I have it on good authority that Bjarni was crushed and almost sliced in two by his own car,' Máki says. 'It's supposed to have been a terrible sight.'

'But why use a car as a murder weapon? Inside a garage?'

'Why not?'

'Don't you think it looks odd?'

'In any case, it's unusual, and it gives me a great headline.'

'I mean, garages are usually full of all sorts of tools that can easily be used to beat someone to death. Why use a car?'

'You mean there's something symbolic about this?'

'Just asking.'

'How did it go? Didn't Bjarni run over one of your clients in that car?' the newshound asks cheerfully.

'Don't go mixing her up in this. She has an alibi.'

'Ah. So you already checked that, did you?'

Máki laughs down the phone.

A day without laughter is a day without sunshine, as Mother said.

41

The pots and pans revolution has begun on Austurvöllur. Thousands of furious victims of the bank collapse have gathered in front of Parliament. They're banging steel and aluminium pots and pans in a desperate attempt to rouse the politicians who presided from dreamland over the crash.

The noise is overwhelming. It's the same inside, where members of Parliament turn up for the business of the day after the Christmas break, as clueless as they were before.

The blackbirds are out in force.

They're supposed to throw a ring of steel around the powerbrokers inside Parliament, protected by helmets and riot shields. The batons, pepper spray and tear gas are there to overpower those unable to contain their justifiable fury. These are the people who are 'starting a riot', as Freyja Dögg put it the other day.

I accompany Ilona to her meeting with the cops and make her describe her unpleasant experience at Efstakot, in every detail.

Ilona confirms once again that Glúmur tricked her into going up to Borgarfjörður with the promise of a hefty payday. But he then left her there as a prisoner.

Her testimony should be more than enough to convince any judge that Glúmur should be remanded in custody, for a long spell, just like the two Lithuanians arrested at Efstakot.

We part later in the day.

Ilona goes with Ludmilla to Keflavík airport, on her way to Scandinavia. I take the silver steed and head out of the city and eastwards to meet Robertas.

He's surprised to see that I haven't brought an interpreter.

'That's deliberate,' I tell him in English. 'Ilona told me that you speak pretty good English.'

His face remains expressionless.

'Ilona has been freed from captivity. She was being held by your friends from Lithuania,' I continue. 'She asked me to give you her love.'

He stares for a long time into my eyes. It's like he's weighing up how trustworthy I am.

'How is she?' he finally asks, in English.

'Better than could be expected after that miserable stay at Efstakot. But she seems more worried about you than herself.'

Robertas smiles faintly.

'Were they arrested?'

'Yes. The Lithuanians are in custody for five weeks,' I say. 'I expect Glúmur will be there as well later today. Tomorrow at the latest.'

'So they have him?'

'Ilona has testified against him. So should you. For both your sakes.'

Robertas asks what options there might be to reduce the number of years he'll have to spend in an Icelandic prison, if he testifies against Glúmur. That's who he came to meet in October, to prepare for the speed factory at Efstakot.

We go over the situation in detail. We make notes of his offer to the city's finest.

On the way home I listen to the hysterical news reports on the radio about the bitter altercations outside Parliament. That all got going when the blackbirds charged out of the Parliament building, supposedly to push protestors back from the tasteless glass cupola that was erected a few years ago, along the western side of the nineteenth-century building.

The newsreader states that many of the protestors have become victims of the blackbirds' pepper spray and batons. Some have been arrested.

My thoughts go immediately to Freyja Dögg. I'm as sure as I can be that she'll be at the centre of all this – even with one arm in a sling.

I roll westwards along the coast road, and park the silver steed by the old harbour. I walk towards the noise.

Protestors have lit a fire on Austurvöllur, probably to keep themselves warm.

Others continue to batter pots and pans, drums and barrels. Placards wave. The calls are for the incompetent government to step down – immediately.

Ranks of blackbirds are lined up before Parliament. Shoulder to shoulder.

Their shields, helmets and uniforms leave no doubt that the protestors have been hurling yoghurt, eggs and all sorts at them.

There are no longer electric lights twinkling in the imposing Christmas tree in front of Parliament. It's a gift that Norwegians every year send to their Icelandic cousins. It's a symbol of peace and understanding in the centre of Reykjavík.

The air around the Norwegian tree is heavy with the harsh stench of pepper spray; the blackbirds haven't been sparing with it in their efforts to clear the most determined protestors from the corridors of power. Here and there protestors who got poison sprayed in their faces are still being tended.

I can't find Freyja Dögg.

First I search through the crowd in front of Parliament, but don't see her anywhere. Then I make for the loudest calls and shouts that are coming from the garden behind the Parliament building. I push through the crowd until agitated boys in black stop me, some of them brandishing batons. Others brandish cans of pepper spray. All of them have frantic eyes.

At the far side of the garden a pile of protestors lie in a heap on the cold ground. They appear to have had their hands tied.

'Who's in charge here?' I yell.

One of the blackbirds points to a tall inspector standing a little to one side.

I try to convince him that I'm looking for my client, who is injured and could be among those arrested.

This copper's not interested in listening to me.

'These people have been arrested for breaching the peace and they're going to the cells,' he raps. 'You can meet your client there tonight or tomorrow.'

'Stella! Stella!'

The call comes from the far side of the garden.

I see Freyja Dögg's silhouette. She's lying on the grass, hands tied.

'The girl has a broken arm,' I yell. 'Let me help her.'

'Back off,' the blackbird snarls, raising his baton.

But I'm not giving up. I keep working on the inspector who seems to exhibit more self-control than his men do. Finally I convince him that it's in his interest to let me help their injured prisoner.

He takes me over to Freyja Dögg, and allows her to sit up.

I look into her beautiful eyes. The pepper spray has left them red and swollen.

'How's your arm?'

'They dislocated my shoulder when they tied me up,' she replies, holding back a sob.

After a while he agrees to cut the plastic strap around her wrists. But he flatly refuses to let me take Freyja Dögg away.

'She gets no special treatment,' he says. 'You'll just have

to wait like everyone else and talk to your client at the station.'

The blackbirds hustle the prisoners in the garden to their feet. They take them, still tied, into the basement of the Parliament building. From there secret passages run in all directions. Ideal escape routes for powerful men frightened of their own people.

The inspector escorts me back through the line of blackbirds.

A pleasant smell of burning pine branches greets me.

Some of the protestors have managed to fell the Norwegian Christmas tree. They haul it triumphantly to the bonfire that in a moment flares up to new heights.

All the same, the foul reek of pepper spray and tear gas lies like a blanket over Austurvöllur. Are these Iceland's death throes? Or what?

42

Wednesday 21ˢᵗ January

The cops have brought Sverrir Guðbjartsson from prison out in the east.

He's in a bad way mentally after being in solitary confinement at Litla-Hraun. He's had neither dope nor freedom for a week. He's been alone with his pain.

Sverrir's mind wanders. His answers are uncertain, even to the simplest questions.

'This man's in a terrible state,' I say. 'Has he had a medical examination?'

'The doctor checked Sverrir this morning and said he was fit to be questioned,' Raggi replies, handing me a standard medical certificate from a doctor I've never heard of.

Sverrir's abrupt movements are all you need to see to know that his nerves are in a wretched state. This has got worse by the day as withdrawal symptoms kick in hard.

The corpulent cop asks repeatedly about his relationship with Sveinfríður Tómasdóttir, going all the way back to primary school.

He gets my client to admit that they've been lovers for some time, and occasionally used drugs together.

On the other hand, Sverrir flatly denies that Sveinfríður has taken any part in the many thefts and break-ins of which he's guilty, and which have fuelled his drug habit.

Raggi's not having that.

'When did she first suggest robbing the church at Bessastaðir?' he asks.

'She's never said a word about that.'

'Did Sveinfríður put you onto there being valuable items in the church? Old stuff that you could sell for a decent wedge of money?'

'No.'

'There were a lot of people at Bessastaðir the day you robbed the church, so it was easy for you to hide in the crowd,' Raggi continues. 'Didn't Sveinfríður pick that as the perfect time to steal the candlesticks?'

'I just wanted to see Sveinfríður, that's why I went out there,' Sverrir stammers. 'That's all there is to it.'

'Did she tell you when the security camera would be switched off?'

'What camera?'

'Did she tell you at what time of day it would be safe to go into the church? Because she had disconnected the CCTV?'

'I never went into the church.'

Fat Raggi ignores everything Sverrir says, as he did before. He just starts all over again. It's the same questions again and again, worded slightly differently.

Sverrir's replies become increasingly slurred. But he continues to deny that he stole from the church, or that Sveinfríður was involved in such a crime.

Eventually, I've had enough.

'This isn't right, hammering away at a sick man.'

Raggi wrinkles his nose.

'Despite his condition, Sverrir has steadfastly denied any wrongdoing,' I continue. 'You'll just have to accept that.'

'Considering the candlesticks were found at your client's home, we're not prepared to accept his ridiculous denials,' Raggi replies. 'Neither will the judge.'

'I'd like to remind you that Sverrir Guðbjartsson is not

on remand for stealing silverware, but for your suspicion that he murdered Benedikt Björgúlfsson. How about producing some real evidence of that? If there is any.'

'We have the analysis of the blood spots found in Sveinfríður's car,' Raggi answers. 'It's Benedikt's blood group, as is the blood found on the Fuhrmann candlestick that was found under your client's bed. That's clear enough. No more evidence required.'

'You have nothing to prove that my client went into the church.'

'Although it appears that Sveinfríður switched off the security camera, there's other convincing evidence. Sverrir was at the location when the murder was committed. The murder weapon was found in his possession and it was covered in the deceased's blood. That'll do to get a conviction.'

'His fingerprints are not on the murder weapon, and are nowhere to be seen inside the church. You're not able to prove that he attacked Benedikt with the candlestick.'

'The likelihood is overwhelmingly strong.'

'According to the police report, the door of my client's room on Hverfisgata was unlocked when the police forced their way in and found him drugged and unconscious,' I continue. 'Anyone could have placed the candlesticks under the bed. Quite possibly the mysterious informer who told you to go there on the false premise that there were drugs to be found. And of course you didn't find any.'

'You can keep that speech for when the case comes up before the judge again,' the fat cop replies, and starts collecting his paperwork.

I feel a need to voice my concerns once more about Sverrir's health.

'He needs to be watched carefully over the coming days.'

'I've every confidence in the staff at Litla-Hraun to assess any need for medical assistance,' Raggi says. 'They make decisions like that every single day.'

He marches out into the passage.

I'm in no mood to let him get away that easily.

I follow Raggi to his office, planting myself in one of the uncomfortable chairs in front of his desk. I wait impatiently for him to take a seat facing me.

'Surely you can see there's something fishy about all this?' I say.

'The only thing that's fishy is that your client won't admit what's blindingly obvious,' the fat cop retorts.

'Did you check out that Japanese card?'

'That's irrelevant.'

'Do you know what those symbols mean?'

'I'm given to understand that in Japan there are loads of gift shops selling cards just like that. Benedikt was there on a business trip before Christmas.'

'Revenge.'

'Revenge, what?'

'Those Japanese symbols signify revenge.'

'And what about it?'

'Someone could have sent the card to Benedikt, as a threat.'

Raggi shakes his head.

'There's nothing to say that Benedikt didn't buy the card himself during his last trip to Japan.'

'Can you prove he bought the card?'

'We're not wasting our time on that kind of stupidity.'

He's clearly in no mood to budge.

'Don't you think it's strange that Benedikt's friend and business partner should be murdered at his place in Selfoss after the wake?'

'It goes without saying that it's unusual for two such influential men to be murdered, let alone in the same month,' Raggi replies. 'But there are no indications of links between the two murders.'

'Are you sure about that?'

'Yes, that's obvious. We know who was responsible for

the murder in the church at Bessastaðir, and that person was in a cell when Bjarni Bjarnason was murdered.'

'It seems to me far more likely that the same person committed both murders. Not least because of the personal and financial links between Benedikt and Bjarni.'

'Murder is a straightforward crime in which the guilty party in most instances is off their head on booze or drugs, just like your client. That's the way it is, even if certain high-profile legal eagles consider it in their interest to muddy the waters.'

I give up, get to my feet. I'm at the door.

I look over my shoulder from the doorway. Raggi's attention is on the computer.

'Listen...'

'What?' he says, without looking up from the screen.

'Did you happen to find a similar Japanese card among Bjarni's effects?'

Raggi yelps with laughter.

'I never expected to see you clutching at straws like this, my dear Stella. But there's a first time for everything.'

'Well?' I demand.

'The Selfoss murder isn't anything to do with me, fortunately.'

'Will you check it out? For me?'

The fat cop waves me out of the door without replying.

43

At last. Glúmur Aðalsteinsson is behind bars.

Right after the District Court's ruling that he should be remanded in custody, the Reykjavík Police Commissioner sent a short press release to the media. This retracted the force's previous accusations that had been levelled at me and Máki. The explanation was that these had been based on now discredited evidence.

But he didn't have it in him to add an apology.

'I've never seen anyone worm their way of out something quite so pathetically,' Máki said. 'But what do you expect from someone who prefers to believe scumbags like Porno Valdi when justifiable accusations are made against his own people?'

Lísa Björk has been busy, as always.

'I managed to get information from the Statistics Authority listing women born on 25th May 1971. There are five of them living.'

She hands me a printout.

There are five women who share the same birthday as Ásthildur, the child who sometime in late 1972 disappeared from the national register, and from the face of the earth.

They live in a variety of places. One's in Ísafjörður. Another lives in Hvammstangi. The third lives in Akureyri. The fourth is in the Westman Islands. Number five lives in Garðabær.

The Garðabær woman is the only one I've ever heard of.

Sandra Ósk Sigurgeirsdóttir. The MP. Freyja Dögg's mother.

'You can presumably cross Sandra Ósk off the list,' Lísa Björk says.

'Why?'

'Because her parents were in the spotlight for years. He was an ambassador posted overseas and she was a children's author. It would be difficult for people like that to keep something of that nature quiet.'

'Then we'll concentrate on the first four to begin with. Would you look into it?'

'No problem.'

I arrange to meet Rósalind at lunchtime.

We meet in the parking lot at Nauthólsvík. It's above the specially designed bathing beach that buzzes with life and fun during the summer. Right now it's cloaked in winter gloom.

Rósalind is very relieved that Glúmur has been arrested.

'But Aðalsteinn is furious that he's been suspended, even though he's on full pay,' she says as we jog westwards along the fence around the runways at Fossvogur.

She's untied the band holding her long red hair. It flows free past her face and over her shoulders.

'But not about his son?'

'No, not at all. Aðalsteinn is adamant that it's all a conspiracy staged by foreign criminals against him and his boy. He's told his pals at the station that he was the one who took on these two Lithuanians to look after the horses at Efstakot, and neither he nor Glúmur suspected that they were abusing their position by producing speed tablets there.'

'And I imagine he knew nothing about Ilona being held there?'

'Nope. Aðalsteinn says it's just not true that Glúmur drove her up there, and she's in cahoots with this foreign mafia that's trying to get out of all this by spreading lies about innocent Icelanders.'

'He surely can't believe his own bullshit?'

'I can tell you that nobody at the station does. A lot of people even find it hard to believe that Aðalsteinn didn't know about the speed factory, considering he spent so much time with the horses at Efstakot last summer and autumn.'

Half an hour later we stroll back towards the parking lot. We pause a few times, and look out over windblown Fossvogur, and the sea that fades into the distant horizon to the west.

We catch each other's eye once or twice. We laugh about nothing in particular. We're like a pair of love-struck teens. Her green eyes sparkle when I invite her to my place on Friday evening.

Mmm!

Lísa Björk has had plenty on her plate while I was out of the office.

'Eygló Arnardóttir called this morning to let you know that she'll be spending a few days with her sister in Mosfellsbær.'

'She's here in the south?'

'Yes, and she'd prefer to meet you today as she has a doctor's appointment tomorrow.'

'That's fine. I'll go and see her this afternoon.'

I can't stop running over the conversation with Raggi in my mind. That's especially because of how smartly he quashed my suggestion that the two murders might be connected.

I'll have to try to uncover the truth myself, to clear my client, since the city's finest say no. I need to find out if there's anything to my suspicions. Or they if might be my imagination.

I'm well aware that I have nothing concrete to work on, just a gut feeling that the two murders must be linked. There has to be an explanation somewhere in Benedikt and

Bjarni's close friendship and intertwined business interests, going all the way back to their schooldays.

That reminds me of the notorious gang of four at the University of Iceland back in the eighties. Half of their number has been murdered. What about the other two? Could they be in danger?

According to Máki, Gunnar Kjartan has been a central pillar of Iceland's political and financial establishment over the last couple of decades. He's the perfect figure pulling strings from behind the scenes with his money and influence. And he was close to Benedikt and Bjarni.

He could be in danger as well, if my still half-formed suspicions are correct.

On the other hand, someone like that isn't likely to tell me a single thing that might be of use. At least, not until I have something solid to work with.

But what about the Reverend Hildibrandur? The lawyer-turned-theologist?

At first glance, he seems a more likely prospect.

As a brand new lawyer, he renounced those long, difficult years of study right after graduating. Instead he went searching for God in dusty tomes.

How come?

I search online for the interview with Reverend Hildibrandur that *Morgunblaðið* ran in 2008. That was the 25-year anniversary of the gang of four graduating in law. I find it easily, and sit back to read.

According to Reverend Hildibrandur, he underwent a life-changing experience in the summer of 1983. That was just after he and his friends graduated from university.

'I didn't experience any sudden epiphany, or enlightenment, as Paul did on the road to Damascus,' he says in the interview. 'Quite the opposite. I experienced a deep trauma, and that trauma led to my questioning the meaning of life, and the point of living any longer. In my desperation I even considered whether or not the right thing to do would be to take my own life, and bring my own sinful existence to an end.'

'And what saved you?' the journalist asks.

'I visited my grandmother, who lives out in the countryside,' Reverend Hildibrandur replies. 'She sensed my unhappiness and one evening she came to my room, where I had laid down to rest, and she handed me a book that she said was the remedy for everything that ails the soul. This was *The Confessions of Saint Augustine*, which recount with honesty his struggle with the sins of this earthly existence and how desperation led him to the only true God. I read all through the night and got up in the morning, not having slept at all, convinced that the only way to atone for my sins would be to follow the example of Augustine, to find God and to serve Him. On returning to Reykjavík, I abandoned the law and entered the theology department of the university.'

The old photos that are alongside the interview in *Morgunblaðið* show the four of them glowing with happiness and confidence. They're dressed the same, in white tuxedos, black ties at their throats. Four grinning young bucks out on the town in the summer of 1983.

The picture must have been taken before the trauma of his sin, the shock that the priest claims hurled him into the darkness of depression.

So what was this terrible sin?

44

Freyja Dögg isn't letting injury, arrest and a grilling by the cops get her down. She gets up and dusts herself off, ready for the next round.

'This incompetent government is on the point of giving up,' she says as I leave her at the National Hospital's A&E department. 'Now we need to keep up the pressure.'

More than likely she's right.

But I have other fish to fry.

Eygló Arnardóttir, former housekeeper at Hvítanes, is staying with her sister in Mosfellsbær. There's a cheerful expression on her face, even though she's in a wheelchair. She's short, and tubby. Her light grey hair is carefully fixed in place, just like that of the master of ceremonies at Bessastaðir.

'I can't get anywhere without help,' she says. 'That's why it's such a disappointment that they postponed the operation.'

Her sister Sólveig is younger, and quick on her feet. She's put coffee cups and a plate piled high with biscuits on the table in the welcoming living room.

The walls are crammed with paintings and photographs of mountains and fjords, and of old houses that look to be uninhabited.

'These are all Guðfríður's pictures from the west,' Eygló explains.

'Guðfríður is my daughter,' Sólveig adds, with a touch of pride.

'I saw a painting from the west on the wall at Jörundur Hákonarson's house,' I say. 'The picture Hjördís Eyjólfsdóttir painted of the farmhouse at Hvítanes in 1970.'

'I remember the picture well,' Eygló replies. 'Hjördís finished working on it just before she returned to Copenhagen.'

'You were that whole summer at Hvítanes?'

'Yes, that's right. That was my fifth summer at Hvítanes. Hákon the elder took me on there for the summer in 1966. When he died, Hákon the younger asked me to stay on. The last year I was housekeeper there was 1975, and that autumn he had all the livestock slaughtered and that was the end of traditional farming there. Hákon's interest was mainly in horses.'

'Tell me about Hjördís.'

Eygló sighs.

'The first time I met her was when Hákon told me to take the jeep to Bíldudalur to fetch the girl who was arriving on the flight from Reykjavík. I remember how dreadful she looked, hardly able to make sense.'

'Because of the drugs?'

'Yes, and as soon as we were home Hákon searched through her suitcase. He found some pills and drugs, and threw the whole lot away, so she got extremely upset and lost control completely, and he had to lock her in the bedroom. It was terrible to see the room when we finally let her out to go to the toilet, because she had hurled everything she could against the door, and had ripped the bedclothes to shreds.'

'Didn't she agree herself to be there to recover?'

'I'm sure she did, but Hjördís was just so ill and in such a bad state that sometimes I don't think she knew what she was doing. One day she made a run for it and she was half-way up the side of the mountain above the farm when she gave up, so Hákon had to practically carry her down. She was in an awful state those first weeks, but then she started to get better, and that was all because of Hákon.'

'In what way?'

'He always had time for Hjördís. Those first few days she frequently had terrible nightmares and he'd sit with her and comfort her, sometimes the whole night long. After three or four weeks she started to show some interest in things other than herself and her illness.'

'Such as painting?'

'That came later. To begin with she became fond of the horses, then she came and helped out with the haymaking, and then she demanded to paint the farmhouse blue.'

I explain to Eygló what Hákon Hákonarson's final wishes were.

She's astonished.

'Hákon never mentioned to me that he was the father of Hjördís's child,' she says.

'Never?'

'No. Of course I could see that their relationship was very close, but I had no idea that she had got pregnant at Hvítanes.'

'They were lovers, though?'

'Yes, there was no hiding that. They often went riding together and I recall that later in the summer when I was going out to the cowshed I saw them returning from an overnight trip and it was obvious what was going on. Of course I knew that she had a husband in Copenhagen, but I felt it was all fine, because I could see how happy Hjördís was and felt that she deserved that after everything she had been through.'

'But you knew nothing about the child?'

'No, nothing. Unfortunately, I never met Hjördís again, even while she was at Jórunnarstaðir,' Eygló replies. 'But I heard tales of what went on there and that Hjördís had become hooked on drugs again. It was obvious that summer of 1972 because Hákon was so deeply troubled.'

'Do you know if he did anything about this?'

'Hákon told me that he'd been over to Jórunnarstaðir and offered her a chance to stay at Hvítanes for the summer, but her husband wouldn't hear of it and his brother told him to get out. I remember that Hákon let fall harsh words about those brothers, who were both hopeless addicts.'

'Was this shortly before Jórunnarstaðir burned down?'

'Yes.'

'What did Hákon have to say about the fire?'

'I don't think that he ever mentioned the fire or Hjördís to me after that.'

'Never?'

'No, I don't think so. And I spent a couple more summers working for him. I had the very strong feeling that after Hjördís took her own life, she became a closed chapter in his life. That's why I never brought her up in conversation, and neither did he.'

I've given the coffee my full attention, but I've barely nibbled at the sugar-sweet biscuits.

'What were your thoughts about Hjördís?' I ask.

'She was a very emotional character and went from one extreme to the other,' Eygló says. 'To be quite honest, I didn't like the look of her to begin with. But that changed once she had shaken off the drugs and I became quite fond of her towards the end. We exchanged pictures before she left and I still have the one she gave me.'

Sólveig fetches a light blue album from a cupboard and lays it in her sister's lap.

'This was the only photo that Hjördís had with her while she was recovering at Hvítanes,' she says. 'It's her confirmation portrait.'

Eygló hands me the black-and-white picture, clearly taken in a studio.

Hjördís's long face is serious. But there's a brightness in her eyes. As there is in her fair hair.

I'm struck.

I've seen this expression of youthful optimism before.
At least, almost.
You can find the past in people's eyes, as Mother said.

45

Thursday 22ⁿᵈ January

The Reverend Hildibrandur shies away from meeting me.

I've been on the phone all evening chasing this man of God. Finally I caught up with him just before midnight. I asked to meet him, and wouldn't take no for an answer. Piled on the pressure until he gave in. He agreed to talk to me early in the morning.

There's a swimming-pool-blue glow to the ceiling of the chapel that was long ago inserted between lecture rooms on the second floor of the University of Iceland's main building.

I used to sneak in here as a student. This was a place to relax after a night on the town. I used to lie on my back on one of the wooden pews. I'd stare up at the pale blue ceiling, and fall fast asleep.

The Reverend Hildibrandur's there before me.

He sits on a pew at the front, deep in something. There's a thick book in his hands.

I'm surprised to see how delicate his face is, almost feminine.

I take a seat at his side. The russet-brown briefcase lies on the pew behind.

He closes the book. His dark eyes take me in.

His brush-cut hair is between grey and white.

'I would like to repeat what I told you yesterday, that I

feel it unbecoming to be discussing Benedikt with the lawyer representing the thug who caused his death in the house of God at Bessastaðir,' he says in a voice that has a certain hoarseness to it.

'There's no certainty that Sverrir Guðbjartsson is guilty.'

'Naturally, you're paid to say that.'

I wave a hand in the direction of the altar rail, and point to screens above the altar encrusted with Iceland crystal. There's gothic lettering, picked out in gold.

'You recall what that says, don't you?' I ask.

'The truth will redeem us.'

'My hope is that the truth will give my client back his freedom.'

Hildibrandur sighs.

'One of my wisest teachers here at the university once said that the truth isn't a stone wall, but a road that we must find and follow, but I probably know less than you do about how the death of my friend occurred.'

'But nobody knew him better than you.'

'That may very well be.'

'I read your interview in *Morgunblaðið*.'

'What interview?'

'The one that was published last year. Along with a picture of the four of you together in the summer of 1983.'

'Ah. That interview.'

'Your friendship has continued, ever since your schooldays?'

'Yes. We all got to know each other at Reykjavík Junior College. We were determined to let nothing wreck our close friendship, and we have been able to keep it that way for many decades.'

'Although you took a different direction to your friends?'

'In our university years we were all determined to seek wealth and fame in business and politics, and Gunnar Kjartan, Bjarni and Benedikt were certainly very successful, but I felt a spiritual need to follow new paths.'

'Why?'

'I suffered a trauma, as I recounted in the interview you mentioned.'

'Yes, I remember. But what was that trauma?'

'That is between me and God.'

'Did your friends know about your falling into sin?'

Hildibrandur hesitates.

'They were fully aware of my mental anguish,' he finally replies.

'And did being born again heal those hurts?'

'I would not go that far, although briefly it did. But my time in this world would have been unbearable without God's mercy and forgiveness.'

'I'd like to know what happened.'

'No.'

There's a heavy silence in the chapel for a while. Then I ask more questions.

'Why do you think your friends were murdered?'

'I know no more about these murders than what the police have stated publicly.'

'I suspect the same person murdered them both.'

The man of God looks up. There's no telling what he's thinking.

'Why?'

'I was hoping that you could point me towards some reason why these two close friends were executed.'

'Executed? It sounds as if you're saying they were punished for some serious wrongdoing.'

I open the briefcase, and get the copy of the Japanese card that was found in Benedikt's jacket pocket.

'Recognise this?'

Hildibrandur's face goes even paler.

'You've seen this before, haven't you?'

He nods.

'Where? From Benedikt?'

'Benedikt flew home the day before his death, and that

evening he called on me.'

'He showed you the card?'

'Yes. He said it had been sent anonymously earlier in the week. He thought it extremely strange, and convinced himself it was a joke of some kind.'

'Was he aware that the symbols on the card are for *fukushuu* – revenge?'

'I told him that.'

'You speak Japanese?'

'It is one of the languages I have studied for many years.'

'Did he take the threat seriously?'

'No. I think not.'

'Why not?'

'He believed it was an aggrieved message from a Japanese business partner who had lost out badly on the bankruptcy of a company they had jointly owned.'

'You agreed with that?'

'At the time it sounded plausible.'

'At the time? But not now?'

The man of God stretches himself, sitting on the wooden pew.

'You have no doubt read in the newspapers that the late Bjarni invited me and Gunnar Kjartan to a wake at his summer residence in Selfoss after Benedikt's funeral at the cathedral,' he says. 'I mentioned the Japanese card that Benedikt had received, and it came to light that Bjarni had received an identical card. That was also sent by post and anonymous.'

Bingo!

'So you can be certain that both Benedikt and Bjarni received similar threats through the post before they were murdered?' I ask.

'Yes. Assuming this was a threat.'

'It's as clear an indication as there could be that the same person committed both murders. The person who sent the cards.'

'The Lord moves in mysterious ways.'

There's something in the man of God's voice that makes me suspicious.

'Meaning what?'

He hesitates for a moment. Then he opens the thick book he's been turning over in his hands the whole time.

'This was in my post box this morning.'

I snatch the envelope. Out drops a light brown card with large black Japanese letters.

'Revenge.'

46

The priest refuses to show the Japanese card to the city's finest.

'I'm convinced this is a serious threat,' I say. 'This signifies that you're the killer's next victim.'

'I find that an almost ridiculous interpretation of a simple postcard,' the Reverend Hildibrandur replies with a faint smile. 'Even if that were the case, I would remind you that my life has been not my own to order for the last few decades. My life belongs to God and its end is entirely in His hands.'

It dawns on me that no rational logic is a match for such faith.

'And what about Gunnar Kjartan?' I ask. 'Do you know if he's received one of these threatening letters?'

'When we came together for the wake in Selfoss he hadn't been aware of having seen a postcard of this nature.'

'He could have received one this week. Just like you.'

'It's possible.'

'Aren't you going to check?'

'I see no reason for that.'

'Why not?'

'I am at one with God and acquiesce to His will.'

'At one with God?' I repeat. 'But not with people?'

'I can assume that not everyone is at one with me, and that is human.'

I stare for a moment at the Reverend Hildibrandur.

'I find your attitude totally beyond understanding,' I tell him at last.

'Do you?'

'Yes. Two of your close friends have been murdered. You could clearly be the murderer's next victim. But you act as if you don't care.'

'I do most certainly care about the deaths of my friends,' he replies. 'But I am weary of life and long for nothing more than to rest in the Lord's keeping.'

'I would call that a weakling's way out, a healthy grown man lying back and waiting to die instead of fighting for his life.'

The man of God gives me a bleak smile.

'I am afraid that there's a world of difference between our outlooks on life.'

'It sounds to me that you're in agreement that this Japanese card could be the precursor to an attempt on your life, and you simply welcome it. Is that it?'

'I am tired.'

'What about your friend? Gunnar Kjartan? Won't you make an effort to look after him?'

'If there's any one person on this earth who's capable of looking after himself, then that man is Gunnar Kjartan,' the man of God replies. 'You need have no concerns about him.'

'I couldn't give a shit about Gunnar Kjartan Vestmann. My only role in this whole case is to look after my client's interests. He's in a cell, suspected of a murder I believe it's unlikely he committed. Do you want his fate on your conscience as well?'

'As well?'

'Yes, because you have something bad on your conscience. That's for sure. There's something for which you've been punishing yourself for the last twenty-five years.'

The Reverend Hildibrandur nods, with reluctance.

I'm not letting up.

'And that Japanese card is somehow linked to the big sin, am I right? The trauma that led to you seeking the Almighty's forgiveness back in the summer of 1983?'

'That would be further proof that the Almighty is omniscient and ubiquitous.'

'So what happened?'

'Vengeance is mine. I will make amends, as the Lord says and I trust His word. What happened and what will happen are between myself and God.'

'So the big sin must be somehow connected to Japan? How?'

The Lord's servant gets slowly to his feet.

'Are you really leaving my client cast adrift?'

'What can I do to help?'

'You could tell me the truth.'

'I have given God my full testimony.'

'That guy doesn't judge murder trials in this city.'

He looks away.

'Your replies remind me of the selfish people in the parable of the Good Samaritan,' I say. 'You're no better than the guy who marched past the injured man without offering a helping hand.'

Hildibrandur's face stiffens.

'Yes,' he intones in a low voice. 'I am that sinful man.'

Despondent, he walks out of the chapel, without another word.

I head back to the office. I can't find it in me to get to grips with the Stella Fund's debts right now. Instead I make repeated attempts to reach Raggi. That's one voicemail after another to call me urgently.

I mull over the Reverend Hildibrandur's confession when I accused him of being the opposite of the Good Samaritan.

'Yes. I am that sinful man.'

Why did he take this comparison of mine so to heart?

Did he walk past someone in need without offering help? In either a practical or a symbolic sense?

Was the young lawyer's trauma in the summer of 1983 something of that nature?

If so, what are the links with Japan?

I call Lísa Björk after mulling things over for a long time. With her, I go over the conversation with Hildibrandur in the university chapel. I ask her to check the national newspapers from April to September 1983.

'I'm interested in any domestic news that's connected in some way to Japan,' I say. 'Especially if there are accidents or deaths that occurred that summer.'

'No problem,' she says. 'Searching for a needle in a haystack is always fun.'

Lísa Björk looks at the screen of her little laptop.

'I've been checking the available family information for those women who were born on 25th May 1971, and I haven't found anything that looks strange.'

'I have a suspicion about Ásthildur.'

She stares at me in astonishment.

'In what way?'

'Yesterday Eygló showed me Hjördís Eyjólfsdóttir's confirmation portrait.'

'And?'

'I've met someone who's the spitting image of her.'

'Who's that?'

'Freyja Dögg.'

47

To my surprise Gunnar Kjartan agrees to meet, even though I played a big part in putting his nephew behind bars.

He lives in a large, two-storey house on Dyngjuvegur. His parents built this white-painted, detached house in the sixties. That's info from Máki.

'Gunnar Kjartan has never had that juvenile nouveau riche urge to show everyone how wealthy he is,' the old newshound reported. 'He's the lion who slinks in the shadows. I reckon it says something about Gunnar Kjartan's temperament that he had tinted glass put in all the windows. Nobody gets to see his wealth without his say-so.'

I park the silver steed by the door. March up to the oak front door. I peer at the little triangle window of stained glass before ringing the bell.

Jónsteinn Ingólfsson comes to the door.

Why am I surprised? Didn't Máki say that Jónsteinn is Gunnar Kjartan's gofer?

He smirks as he opens the cupboard in the hall.

I hand him my coat. But he just jerks his head at the cupboard. It's like he's telling me he's no servant.

'He'll see you in the library.'

Gunnar Kjartan is sitting with a book in the middle of the room. He's a small, plump man in a carved rocking chair. He has chubby cheeks. Dark hair but no beard.

There's a little silver bell on the table at his side. It's on top of a stack of company annual reports.

Dark bookshelves fill all four walls. They're packed with bound volumes. The large floor tiles are meant to mimic a Roman mosaic.

He doesn't get to his feet. But he gestures me to a seat facing him, in a deep black armchair.

'I know all about you,' he says in a voice that's as smooth as silk. 'You've been involved in persecuting my nephew for no good reason.'

'Really?'

He nods.

'Glúmur is a bold lad, but can be impulsive and doesn't tread as cautiously as he should, but he hasn't had any involvement in kidnapping or manufacturing drugs. Absolutely not.'

'The courts will presumably rule on his guilt or innocence.'

'There's no direct evidence against him. The Lithuanian workmen employed by Aðalsteinn at Efstakot have never seen him before, let alone all the rest of it.'

'I didn't come here to talk about Glúmur.'

'You have talent, but you don't make the right use of it.'

'How so?'

'You spend too much time on trivial shitbags. If you had come to me ten or fifteen years ago, you'd be rich by now.'

'Like Benedikt Björgúlfsson and Bjarni Bjarnason?'

'They were outstanding entrepreneurs who knew how to make great things from not very much, and sometimes from nothing at all.'

'And they're both dead.'

Gunnar Kjartan glowers from beneath heavy brows.

'I'm also told that you're a foul-mouthed nymphomaniac who revels in the dregs of society. A veritable Messalina.'

I make an attempt at an amiable smile.

'What do you want from me?' he rasps.

'I've long wanted to see the *éminence grise* in his own surroundings.'

A thin trace of a smile flickers across his thick lips.

'And I had an interesting chat with your friend the Reverend Hildibrandur.'

The smile vanishes.

'This morning he received the same threatening letter as was sent to your comrades a few days before they were murdered.'

'Hildibrandur told me about your visit.'

'Have you received such a threat?'

'I'm not inclined to treat a cheap Japanese postcard as a personal threat.'

'Is that yes or no?'

'The answer to your question is no. Nobody has sent me such a card.'

'Strange.'

'Are you seriously implying that the deaths of my friends were due to someone seeking revenge?' he asks at last.

'Yes.'

'Why?'

'I don't know.'

'Revenge for what?'

'Possibly for whatever you and your friends got up to in the summer of 1983.'

'What did we get up to?' he asks gently. There's no change of expression.

'I don't know. Not yet. But you know, of course.'

'You are very much on the wrong track.'

'Who could have had good reason to murder your friends?'

'The Commissioner of Police informed me last night that I could be in no doubt that your drug addict murdered Benedikt,' Gunnar Kjartan replies.

'So who took Bjarni's life?'

'He's no closer to an answer, unfortunately.'

I cross my legs. Lean back in the chair.

'How about you tell me exactly what happened to you and your friends that summer? So we can start looking for the true killer? And before the Reverend Hildibrandur follows them upstairs?'

Gunnar Kjartan rocks back and forth, deep in thought.

'I can't accept that these Japanese cards had anything at all to do with my friends' deaths,' he says at last. 'But I'm intrigued by your being convinced there is such a connection.'

'Intrigued?'

'Yes. I'm aware that in similar cases of this kind you have been particularly insightful. But that doesn't convince me that you're right on this occasion.'

'You're absolutely not prepared to tell me what happened to you all?'

'We all graduated that spring. All of us started work at legal chambers,' Gunnar Kjartan replies. 'Shortly after that, Hildibrandur heard the call and found redemption.'

'How come he got the call?'

'He didn't tell you himself?'

'He spoke only about a personal trauma. Which naturally means nothing.'

'Hildibrandur suffered a personal trauma, that's true. And he was born again, and we weren't. That alone should be enough to make you doubt that you're on the right track.'

'Your life could be at stake.'

There's a shadow of a smile.

'I'm well looked after by a fine bodyguard,' he says.

I stand up.

'No point continuing playing these games...'

Gunnar Kjartan rings the silver bell. Jónsteinn immediately opens the door.

'...But I felt I should warn you.'

'A beautiful thought can be found in a corrupted body.'

'But never in the ice-cold heart of power,' I snap right back.

Just to have the last word.

48

Friday 23rd January

Raggi's still in doubt.

The fat cop can't deny that the postcards printed with the Japanese *fukushuu* characters were found on both Benedikt and Bjarni.

'The police in Selfoss found another of these cards in Bjarni's jeep,' he finally admits early in the morning. That's when he eventually gets round to answering my string of messages. 'But that tells me nothing.'

'The Reverend Hildibrandur also received one of these cards.'

I briefly recount my conversations with the two surviving members of the gang of four. I do my best to convince him that that these Japanese cards are a clear indication that this servant of the Lord is in danger of his life.

'Unfortunately, Hildibrandur refused my requests for him to take the card he received to the police. That seems to be because he's in the grip of a serious death wish.'

'Did Gunnar Kjartan get one of these wretched cards?'

'He says not.'

'There you go,' Raggi says triumphantly.

'But he has a bodyguard.'

'Who's that?'

'Jónsteinn Ingólfsson.'

Raggi coughs down the phone.

'You know this rascal, don't you?'

'Yep,' the guardian of law and order replies.

I do my best to persuade Raggi to contact the Reverend Hildibrandur. But he sees no reason to trouble the man of God.

'You're just doing your best to wreck the case against Sverrir Guðbjartsson, even though the evidence is right there in front of you,' he says, sounding exhausted.

'I'm urging you to bring in Hildibrandur before it's too late,' I repeat.

'You know, I've more than enough to do with society falling apart without going along with your whims,' Raggi replies. He hangs up without another word.

Ludmilla emailed me earlier, a picture she took of Dagnija and Ilona on Drottninggatan in Stockholm.

Their smiles are warm. According to Ludmilla, they're going back to Latvia for a few weeks for a break.

I'll show the picture to Robertas as soon as I get a chance, when the cops are ready to interrogate him again. I've already let drug squad chief Gunnbjörn know that Robertas met Glúmur Aðalsteinsson when he came to Iceland back in October. He's been told that was a trip to Efstakot to prepare the speed factory.

Austurvöllur's cold this morning, not many people about. Everyone knows the government's shaky foundations are about to come apart because of the protests over the last few weeks. Even some party leaders are openly talking about elections in the spring.

Sandra Ósk comes across as drowning in work at her office.

The MP is professionally groomed, expensively dressed. It looks like she's on the way to yet another official banquet, before her party gets shoved out of office.

'I had hoped that Freyja Dögg and I had seen the last of you,' she says with a chill in her voice. 'Surely you're not still persecuting poor Bjarni beyond the grave?'

'This errand is of a very different nature,' I reply, keeping it cool.

'Make it quick. I don't have much time.'

Last night I was full of doubt about whether to take such a radical step. That's simply because my theory's based solely on looks.

I've not a shred of proof.

The resemblance between Freyja Dögg and Hjördís Eyjólfsdóttir's confirmation portrait could be pure coincidence. There are plenty of examples of people having similar facial features – even doppelgängers – without being related.

It could be a coincidence that Sandra Ósk shares a date of birth with Ásthildur.

That's why I wondered whether to leave Sandra Ósk alone.

But this morning my opinion has changed. I have a duty to make one last effort to respect Hákon Hákonarson's dying wish – to get to the bottom of this. One way or the other.

I take a seat on the sofa facing her desk. Time to go to work.

'A few weeks ago I was asked to find out what became of a roughly one-year-old child called Ásthildur Ásvaldsdóttir.'

'And what's that to do with me?' Sandra Ósk snaps.

'Ásthildur was born in Copenhagen on the 25th of May 1971, the same day as you. She vanished from the official records in late 1972.'

'Vanished, how?'

'I believe she was given a new name and new parents, although there are no records of this.'

'What happened to her parents?'

'Ásthildur's registered parents both died earlier that year, 1972.'

Sandra Ósk shrugs.

'I don't see what you expect me to do.'

'I suspect that you are Ásthildur.'

She stares at me in astonishment.

'I've always known you were crazy,' she says at last. 'But I didn't suspect that you were completely off your head.'

'A simple DNA test would confirm this one way or the other,' I say.

A sudden fury flashes in her eyes.

'Get out!' she shouts, getting to her feet.

'We can discuss this further...'

'Out!'

The MP's assistant looks up from his keyboard as I stumble through the office doors.

'Everything all right?' he asks worriedly.

I shrug, and head out into the cold.

It goes without saying that was the response I could have expected. There's no reason to assume that Sandra Ósk would have the slightest inkling about her real background. That's if she is Ásthildur.

I could be wrong. It happens. Not often, but it does.

That would be a hell of a bummer.

I inhale the invigorating cold air of Austurvöllur. There's none of that lousy tear gas and pepper spray stink. Not for the moment, at any rate.

Hmmm!

For the rest of today I'm not going to think about sulky crims, old men's dying wishes and society's endless dance of death.

Time to live a bit!

I switch off my mobile.

Gradually, I manage to push all the everyday crap to the back of my mind. I'm concentrating instead on preparing tonight's wonderful banquet.

It's the Friday feast for me and Sóley Árdís – and the chick with the green eyes.

49

My daughter has no intention of going to sleep.

She fights her damnedest to stay awake, even though she can barely keep her eyes open.

Finally I give up and put her favourite in the player. The Smurfs have often been the best way to put her to sleep late in the evening.

The evening's feast was a delight. Goose breast gratin, monkfish wrapped in herbs, crème brûlée with blueberries.

And Pinot Grigio. Montalcino's wonderful white wine. Every sip comes with the fresh aroma of an Italian summer.

Rósalind's colourful dress also reminds me of summer, sunshine and brighter days.

She tells me a few funny cop shop stories over dinner. Then she asks straight out if my client's going to plead guilty of the murder at Bessastaðir.

'He's adamant he's innocent,' I reply.

'He doesn't have a chance, does he? Everyone at the station is certain he did it, off his head on drugs.'

'I suspect it's more complex than that.'

'In what way?' she asks.

Those deep green eyes beg me to tell her what I'm thinking.

'I feel there has to be a connection between the two murders. Primarily because they both received the same threat of revenge before they were murdered.'

'You think it's the same perpetrator?'

'Yes. And now another friend of theirs has been sent the same threat.'

'Do you really think the murderer sent Benedikt and Bjarni threats in Japanese, and then killed them? And that the priest is next in line?'

I nod.

'Who?'

'All I can be sure of is that my client was on remand at Litla-Hraun when Bjarni's murder took place.'

'Why a threat in Japanese?'

'Unfortunately, I don't know,' I reply.

'Benedikt has been notorious since the banks collapsed for his part in all that,' she says. 'There have to be plenty of people who lost big time doing business with him, including in Japan.'

'Undoubtedly,' I say. 'But I also suspect that the threats are connected in some way to a trauma that Hildibrandur suffered in the summer of 1983.'

'What trauma?'

I shrug.

'So you don't know that either?' she asks.

'No. Not yet.'

'Or how that trauma could connect to the threatening letters?'

'I'm still searching.'

Rósalind is pensive.

'Could these threatening letters have been sent to divert attention away from the real reason for these killings?'

'Could be. But then they wouldn't be linked to the past of the gang of four.'

'If your theory is correct, why hasn't Gunnar Kjartan received a threatening letter like the other three?'

'I couldn't say. Maybe he's just the last one on the list.'

Rósalind seems to have a sudden inspiration.

'Unless he sent those cards himself?' she says, excited.

'Gunnar Kjartan?'

'Yes. Why not? I know they were all friends and colleagues back in the day, but what do you really know about their relationship over the last few years?'

I think over this unexpected angle.

'Gunnar Kjartan was certainly at the reception at Bessastaðir that day when Benedikt was murdered,' I reply after a pause for thought. 'So was the gofer, Jónsteinn Ingólfsson. His nephew Glúmur was there as well, for that matter. They were all at Bessastaðir that day.'

'Really?'

'Gunnar and Jónsteinn were also at the house in Selfoss shortly before Bjarni's death,' I continue. 'Gunnar told me himself that Jónsteinn drove him back to Reykjavík that night. The question is when? Before the murder – or after?'

'I've heard this Jónsteinn mentioned at the station,' Rósalind says. 'Isn't he some sort of manager at El Dorado?'

'Yes, he works for both Gunnar Kjartan and Porno Valdi.'

'I hear he had a reputation for being heavy-handed when he was calling in debts in the past. Not that anyone went to the police about him.'

'That's quite true. Unfortunately, I have no solid facts to back up all this conjecture. Raggi says I'm just clutching at straws.'

'To get Sverrir off the hook?'

'Yes.'

'Sometimes the simplest answer is the right one.'

'You mean that my client could be guilty?'

She nods.

'These Japanese card threats are the only strong indication that he isn't.'

'And if they have nothing to do with the murder?'

I shake my head.

'Then I'd have to believe in a string of far-fetched

coincidences. Can't do that.'

She sighs.

'In your position I'd focus on Gunnar Kjartan and Jónsteinn.'

'Hmm.'

After dinner I try to introduce Rósalind to ink-black espresso. And a touch of Jack D.

'Spirits don't agree with me,' she smiles. But she sips the dark Tennessee nectar.

We sit side by side on the sofa. Sóley Árdís lies stretched out on the soft blanket in front of the TV.

Rósalind seems reluctant to tell me too much about herself.

'I was lucky, and found a small apartment to rent in the west end of the city when I joined the force,' she says. 'I like being in the centre.'

'You live alone?'

'No. Cleopatra's there with me.'

'Who's Cleopatra?'

'My cat!' Rósalind laughs.

I gently brush the long red locks from her face.

She glances at Sóley Árdís, who is totally engrossed in the Smurfs.

Then she leans closer to me. Closes those deep green eyes.

Her pink lips are hot and moist.

50

Saturday 24th January

Rósalind slipped away early in the morning.

Happy and satisfied, she had fallen asleep in my arms, after a night of passion.

Even so, it got off to a shy start.

'It's the first time I've slept with another woman,' she whispered under the duvet. That was after I'd relieved her of the colourful dress, and her white underwear.

'See it as a new beginning in your life,' I replied.

She let herself be guided, and learned fast to give as well as receive.

Afterwards it was a delight to rest my face in those long red locks. Even though I had found out that she's actually a brunette.

It's a timely reminder that not everything in this world is how it appears.

While I give my little sweetheart breakfast, I think over our conversation last night about the murder at Bessastaðir.

Rósalind has certainly managed to make me doubt.

Am I chasing mirages?

It's possible.

It's Sandra Ósk who breaks into my train of thought.

'Can you meet today?' she asks.

'Of course.'

'I'm at the office until midday. After that I'll be in meetings into the evening.'

'We'll be there shortly.'

'We?'

'My daughter and I. She's two.'

'OK.'

It's odd to get a call from the MP who threw me out yesterday.

What's changed?

Sandra Ósk is immaculate, as always. But her face shows she's tired. Her eyes are puffy. It's as if she hasn't slept.

'Your visit yesterday took me completely by surprise,' she says, showing me to the sofa. 'That's why I lost my temper. Fortunately, that rarely happens.'

'No problem.'

Sóley Árdís immediately starts exploring the office.

'I would like to ask you who requested that you search for this Ásthildur.'

'That's no secret,' I reply. 'His name was Hákon Hákonarson and for most of his life he was a horse breeder in the Westfjords.'

'Was?'

'Yes. Hákon is deceased. This was his dying wish.'

'What was behind this?'

'Hákon believed that he was Ásthildur's father.'

'She was Ásvaldsdóttir. That's what you told me.'

'Hjördís Eyjólfsdóttir was married to Ásvaldur Rögnvaldsson. But she spent the summer of 1970 at Hvítanes by Arnarfjörður with Hákon. And Ásthildur was born nine months later.'

Sandra Ósk looks me straight in the eye.

'I assume everything between us remains confidential?'

'If that's what you want.'

'I insist.'

'Fine.'

'I have always believed that my mother and father were

my biological parents. I've never had the slightest reason to think otherwise.'

'That applies to most of us.'

'My parents were at the embassy in New York when I was born and always told me I was born there,' she continues. 'That's why I found your suggestion so ridiculous.'

I glance quickly at Sóley Árdís. She's crawled under the desk.

'But last night I told my parents about your visit...'

Sandra Ósk hesitates.

'And the story changed?'

'Yes. They adopted me when I was a year old.'

'Just like Ásthildur.'

'Mum and Dad were allowed to adopt me on the condition that they asked no questions about my background. So they have no idea if I could be this Ásthildur or not.'

'I understand.'

'It was the banker Rögnvaldur Hermannsson who arranged this.'

'Ásthildur's grandfather.'

'Yes. He was a good friend of my parents at that time. I often saw him in New York when I was a child.'

'In that case I think it's all clear.'

Sandra Ósk sits up straighter in her chair.

'I intend to ask Rögnvaldur myself about my origins,' she says.

'Then you should find out the truth.'

'I would like to stress that this remains confidential.'

'It's up to you.'

'Exactly.'

'But I would appreciate it if you could let me know how this concludes.'

'We'll see how it plays out,' Sandra Ósk says, getting to her feet. 'But remember that this is and will remain a secret between us.'

'Aren't you curious to know more about Hjördís and Hákon?'

'I don't know. This has all been so sudden,' she replies. 'I was always taught to live in the moment. My father always said that the past was a place for dusty academics.'

'Come on,' I say to my daughter.

We go hand in hand out onto Austurvöllur, where thousands have gathered to put the government out of its misery.

The present is the past's nightmare, as Mother said.

51

Sunday 25th January

Bjarni Bjarnason was buried this morning.

'Not as many politicos there as I'd expected,' reported Máki, who had been at the funeral in Selfoss. There was a story and a picture on the *News Blog*. 'They're probably all too busy stabbing each other in the back amidst the ruins of the government.'

At midday, I see an email from Lísa Björk.

Yesterday I went through all the Icelandic newspapers for the summer of 1983. There are just two stories that have a connection to Japan. One is a long article about Asian attitudes to grief. The other one is about a man of Asian ancestry who was involved in an accident in the south of Iceland when a car rolled over.

I quickly scan the links she's sent me.

My attention's on a stripped back account of a traffic accident that occurred near the lake at Thingvellir in June 1983.

Some people noticed that a car had come off the gravel road and crashed down a steep rock face. They hurried to the nearest farm and called the Selfoss police. The boys in black arrived half an hour later and they found a couple in their thirties in the wreck, a man of Japanese ancestry and his wife. Both were unconscious and seriously injured.

It took the rescue team a long time to extricate them

from the wreckage of the car.

A terrible accident. But just an accident. At least, going by the news report.

It's not the kind of event I'm searching for. At best, it's another straw to clutch at.

All the same, I reach for the phone. I get hold of the former chief inspector who was on the Selfoss force. He's an eighty-year-old man who spent a quarter of a century working for the District Commissioner's office. Now he lives in an old people's home, Hrafnista in Hafnarfjörður.

'You're not asking for much are you, my dear lady?' he says over the phone. 'Have you any idea how many traffic accidents there are every year in the Selfoss district?'

'No.'

'Serious accidents can run into the dozens. But there can be hundreds of accidents altogether.'

'This accident that *Morgunblaðið* reported doesn't ring any bells?'

'I can't say it does.'

'Where do I get hold of police reports from that time?'

'I couldn't tell you, dear lady. I left the police more than a decade ago,' the oldster replies. 'But I remember that when computers took over at our station, all the old paper stuff was boxed up and put in storage somewhere in the town. That's all I can tell you.'

'I need to speak to someone who was on the scene there in 1983.'

'Good luck, my dear.'

'Could you help me out? Maybe call any old colleagues? Ask if any of them remember this accident?'

'I suppose I could,' he says. 'But don't expect miracles.'

Straws. Miracles.

But the old boy takes me by surprise.

It's dinner time when he calls, just when I'm watching the impending collapse of the government on the TV news, and the informal talks about a minority administration that'll keep ministers' chairs warm until elections in the spring.

'The man's name is Jón Gíslason,' he says, straight to the point. 'He was a temporary constable with us in 1983. He was one of those who attended the scene and remembers it well.'

'Brilliant!'

'Jón moved to Reykjavík. He joined the fire service, and he's still there.'

The old boy reels off Jón Gíslason's number, and I call right away. I invite him round for coffee this evening.

He's tall, slim and muscular. Fair hair, blue eyes.

He's quite something. Even though he's pushing sixty.

Jón makes himself comfortable on the sofa in the living room. And he appreciates the coffee.

'Why the interest in this car crash?' he asks.

'I'm searching for those who were hurt in the crash, or their descendants.'

'I see. I can't say I know anything about the family.'

'But you were at the scene?'

'I was. It wasn't a pretty sight. That's why it's so clear in my memory.'

'What happened?'

'The car had come off the road on a blind hill and it must have crashed twenty, thirty metres down a steep slope. It was rocky, with stony ground and sheer rock faces, so it was a struggle to get our equipment down to the car. We had to cut away part of the wreck to get the people out, and they were both seriously injured and unconscious.'

'Who were these people?'

'There was something about it in the papers, I think,' Jón says. 'Probably after the driver died.'

'He died?'

'Yes, that's right. As far as I recall, he was a long time in a coma in hospital.'

'How long?'

'I couldn't say. But there was definitely something about him in the papers, because he was a scientist.'

'A scientist?'

'That's it. I think he was studying volcanic activity, or something like that.'

'A Japanese volcanologist?'

'Yes, he was Japanese, that's right. But he was also Icelandic, as far as I know.'

'Brilliant.'

'His wife took a long time to recover,' Jón continues. 'I recall that she didn't regain consciousness until sometime after her husband had died, and she was left seriously disabled. I don't know if she made any more of a recovery after that.'

'It was definitely an accident?'

Jón's clear blue eyes stare back at me.

'I had a feeling that you'd ask about that,' he replies quietly.

'Why's that?'

'I heard it mentioned a year or so later, after the woman had regained consciousness, that she said a Range Rover had forced them off the road.'

'Really? Was that investigated?'

'There's nothing I can tell you from first-hand knowledge, because I'd left the force by then. I was only a temporary officer there in Selfoss. But as far as I recall, by the time the woman came around, the wreck had been scrapped.'

'And with it any chance of proving if there might have been a collision?'

'Exactly.'

I ply Jón with more questions, until I'm certain there's no more he can tell me about the car accident that took place on the Grafninginn road in June 1983.

Then it's the internet, to search for the Japanese scientist. He'd been unconscious for more than six months.

The day his funeral took place in the chapel in Fossvogur, a fellow geologist at the University of Iceland recounted his career in an obituary in *Morgunblaðið*.

Tomio was of Japanese descent, but had taken Tómas as his Icelandic name. He was just forty when he died. He had come to Iceland as a young man to study volcanology, met geologist Dagrún Sveinsdóttir, and married her.

There was no mention of any children, neither in the article nor in any of the family notices.

Had they been childless? No vengeful descendant?

Hell!

52

Monday 25th January

The next morning goes into serving the needs of Mammon. The Stella Fund needs a shot in the arm.

I need to chase up debts, negotiate contracts with creditors and with debtors who can't pay on time. I need to give the stocks and shares lad precise instructions on what to buy and sell in the next few days.

After the conversation with Jón Gíslason at the weekend I get the feeling that we're getting somewhere. There's a straightforward enough reason. The fireman's account indicated unequivocally that the accident near the lake at Thingvellir in June 1983 didn't happen by itself.

Did the gang of four have anything to do with it? Was this fatal accident the trauma that sent Hildibrandur to throw himself on the Lord's mercy in the hope of redemption?

If so, this tragic incident could have been the trigger behind the murders. This could be the reason why the killer sent the Japanese cards to Benedikt, Bjarni and Hildibrandur. These sent clear messages that the time of reckoning was at hand.

That's why this morning I asked Lísa Björk to find out everything she could about Dagrún Sveinsdóttir and her relations – especially siblings. Also any connection with her husband's family in Japan needed to be clarified, or if there might be any of Tómas's relatives resident in Iceland.

'This murder took place around a quarter of a century ago,' she said doubtfully. 'Why would someone want to seek revenge now?'

'I'm fully aware that if this is about revenge for Tómas's death, then it's very late in the day,' I reply. 'But we need to check every possibility. This is the only option left that could take us forward.'

Lísa Björk brings me her report on the day's activity shortly before I head to the nursery to collect my daughter.

'Who told you they were childless?' she asks.

'It was in Tómas's obituary in *Morgunblaðið*.'

'Ah, what am I thinking? He died before the birth.'

'What birth?'

'Dagrún was pregnant when the accident occurred.'

'Is that so?'

'The crash left her crippled, and she still is. But the child was born by caesarean section in February, the 23rd February 1984, to be precise. She had a daughter who was christened Tómasína, after her late father. I understand that Dagrún's sister has been mainly responsible for her upbringing.'

'So she'll turn twenty-five next month?'

'Correct.'

'Is Dagrún's sister prepared to talk to us?'

'No. I got an angry response when I called and mentioned the accident, and she hung up on me.'

'That's a shame.'

Lísa Björk looks up from the screen.

'I still haven't tried to get in touch with Tómasína,' she says. 'I thought that might not be advisable at this stage, in case she could be the perpetrator.'

I nod my agreement.

'It's as well to tread carefully.'

'Dagrún lived for a long time in sheltered accommodation on Hátún, but last year she suffered a stroke and has been in a hostel in Grafarvogur since then,'

Lísa Björk adds. 'I understand that Dagrún is more or less out of it and there's no point trying to contact her. Tómasína has a habit of visiting her mother once a week, generally on Wednesdays.'

'Anything on Tómas's Japanese family?'

'Nobody I've spoken to is aware of any of Tómas's Japanese relatives being resident in Iceland.'

'That's excellent work,' I say. 'Next step is to gather all the information we can about the girl. What was her name again?'

'Tómasína.'

'OK. That can wait until tomorrow.'

I'm on the way out of the door when the name hits me. Tómasína?

'Where have I heard that name before?'

Lísa Björk looks at me with wide, questioning eyes.

'I don't think you've ever mentioned any Tómasína to me,' she says.

I stop in the corridor. I'm doing everything I can to dig deep into my memory.

'I haven't heard it...' I call out. 'Seen it. I've seen the name somewhere. Where?' I glance at the clock. 'Hell! I'm late!'

Walking to the nursery, I pummel my memory to give up what it's keeping back. But the light doesn't go on until I'm parking in the drive outside the red town house.

I shepherd Sóley Árdís ahead of me into the office, shutting the door behind me. Hurriedly, I leaf through the red folder that contains copies of the main witness statements in Sverrir Guðbjartsson's case. I haul out the police report, and stare in triumph at the full name of the witness entered in the front page by the boys in black.

'I knew it!'

Sveinfríður!

My suspected murderer client's girlfriend.

Sveinfríður Tómasína Tómasdóttir.

53

Tuesday 26th January

Guilty or not, if his friend Sveinfríður was really the one behind the murder in the church at Bessastaðir, then my client is in it up to his neck.

Could she have persuaded Sverrir to murder Benedikt Björgúlfsson? Did she simply get him to cover up the crime? Or did she pick him out from the outset as the scapegoat?

I'm heading out east in the silver steed, hunting for the truth.

Sverrir has clearly been given sedatives to calm him down. His movements are sluggish and weak, and there's a dazed look in his eyes.

I have to repeat a few questions to get answers.

He says he first got to know Sveinfríður at college in Reykjavík. They became good friends there, taking part in the social scene as they both had a strong interest in drama and dance.

They frequently went out together during those years, going from one bar or disco to the next, far into the night. They played around with ecstasy, and later other drugs.

'I always seemed to need bigger and bigger hits to hit the spot, but Sveinfríður always knew when to stop,' he says. 'She's so smart.'

'Did you often go to her place?'

'Just the first few months. Then her aunt found out we'd been trying ecstasy and I was banned after that.'

'Where did you meet after that?'

'We were in the same year at college, so we went to my place a few times. Otherwise we just had fun downtown.'

'Why did Sveinfríður live with her aunt?'

'That's because her mother was seriously disabled.'

'Do you know what happened to her?'

'Yeah, she was in a car accident. That was when Sveinfríður's father died.'

'Did she often talk about her father?

'Sometimes, when she'd been in touch with relatives in Japan.'

Then it's time to move on to the theft and the murder at the Bessastaðir church.

'Before we go any further, I'd like to remind you yet again that you have to think of yourself and nobody else, not even your friend Sveinfríður,' I say. 'Otherwise you're going to be locked up here for many, many years.'

'I haven't done anything.'

'What made you decide to go to Bessastaðir that particular day?' I ask, as my client thinks it over for a while. 'The whole truth. Otherwise I can't help you.'

'All right,' he says at last. 'Sveinfríður called around midday.'

'What for?'

'She said she had some gear for me.'

'What was that?'

'Amphetamine.'

'So you went out to Bessastaðir to get some speed from Sveinfríður?'

'Yes.'

'And she told you to wait in the car?'

'Yeah, she couldn't get away when I got there, so she told me to go out to the car.'

'Did she mention the church?'

'She just said the car was outside the church.'

'Nothing else?'

'Nothing.'

'She said nothing about candlesticks in the church? Or any other items that could be stolen?'

'No. Nothing.'

'How long were you asleep in the car?'

'I think I must have been asleep there the whole time,' he replies. 'I remember lying on the back seat to rest and I dozed off. Sveinfríður was driving to town when I woke up.'

'Absolutely sure?'

'Yes, that's the truth of it.'

'All right. Is Sveinfríður your girlfriend?'

Sverrir stares back with dead eyes.

'There was never anything permanent between us.'

'Meaning what?'

'That it was just something that happened, when it felt right.'

'It, what? Sex?'

'Yeah.'

'But you're in love with her, aren't you?'

'Could be. But Sveinfríður's with someone.'

'She has another guy?'

'Yep, that's why I knew I never had a real chance there.'

'You mean they've been together a long time?'

'Yes.'

'What's his name?'

'The boyfriend?'

'Yes.'

Sverrir replies with a despondent shrug.

'You don't know his name?'

'I never wanted to be around them together,' he says.

'But you know who he is?'

'The Rock.'

'What?'

'She calls him her Rock.'

'Her Rock? But doesn't he have a name?'

His eyes close. He's clearly had enough.

'Come on,' I say. 'Just one more question.'

Sverrir nods without looking up.

'You had to spend at least two hours waiting in Sveinfríður's car. You're sure you didn't see anyone go into the Bessastaðir church all that time? Or come out of the church?'

I'm carefully watching my client's face.

His eyes snap open. There's a look of surprise. It's as if something unexpected has appeared from the depths of his memory.

'No,' he says, his voice mechanical, as if speaking to himself. 'No.'

'No, what?'

His eyes close again. He slumps forward over the table.

'Nobody,' he mumbles. 'Saw nobody, nobody at all.'

Total bullshit.

The wretched kid is lying to me. No doubt about it.

Who's he protecting?

54

I've no longer the slightest doubt that there's a cold-blooded killer hiding behind Sverrir Guðbjartsson. I tell him that, straight out.

Even so, he doesn't seem to understand the seriousness of the situation. He continues to deny having seen anyone go into the church at Bessastaðir around the time Benedikt Björgúlfsson was murdered, or come out.

I tell him repeatedly that he can no longer afford to tell lies to shield someone else, but it's not sinking in. He just shakes his head.

Sheesh!

Clients can be as stubborn as mules sometimes.

I take the quickest route back to the city. I listen to the news on the radio of negotiations for the formation of a new government that's supposed to be in the works.

I switch off the radio as the phone rings.

'Do you know how come Glúmur is no longer on remand?' Máki asks.

I can't believe what the old newshound is saying. Unexpected, but true.

'That's out of the question,' I reply.

'My sources are certain that Glúmur is a free man.'

'They can't let him out,' I protest. 'He's a kidnapper!'

'But they have.'

'Fuck!'

I end the call and try drug squad supremo Gunnbjörn

Hannesson, and Raggi the fat cop. I'm told they're both unavailable.

Finally I call the Reykjavík District Court. It's confirmed that the remand order for Glúmur was reversed that morning.

'Why the hell's that happened?'

'New evidence,' replies the apparatchik on the other end.

'What new evidence?'

'It's not my place to say.'

Hell!

What a spineless jobsworth.

It didn't even cross my mind that the system's big beasts would go so far as to shred Ilona's evidence. But I realise this has to be what's happened.

Gunnar Kjartan has exerted his influence. The tentacles of power doing their thing.

I recall that the man had assured me the Lithuanians arrested at Efstakot had refused to admit to recognising Glúmur, let alone all the rest of it.

Then it's their word against Ilona's.

But Robertas knew better. He had met these two Lithuanians at Efstakot in October, that time Glúmur drove him up-country.

And Gunnbjörn knows perfectly well that Robertas is prepared to testify to this in court. So why wasn't he questioned again, before Glúmur was released?

The drug squad chief had also heard Svanhvít's testimony. That includes her having passed messages about Ilona from Glúmur to Robertas who's on remand.

What the hell's going on?

My suspicious nature is going into overdrive.

Gunnar Kjartan and his brother-in-law Aðalsteinn are both at the heart of the establishment power hierarchy. No doubt they've been able to pull hard at strings behind the scenes. All the same, I still can't believe they've been able to get their way.

Lísa Björk greets me at the office with a smile on her face.

'What now?' I ask. I'm trying to contain my rage, which shouldn't be inflicted on my wonderful colleague.

'Some unexpected information just now,' she says, perching on the front of her desk with the little laptop in her hands.

'Let's hear it.'

'I know one of the nursing staff at the hostel where Dagrún has been a patient since November,' she says. 'So I took her out to lunch.'

'Good move.'

'She told me that many of the patients at the hostel are more or less abandoned by their families, especially those who are mentally in such a bad way that they don't recognise their closest relatives.'

'Hmm.'

'But she said that Dagrún's fortunate in that her sister and daughter visit regularly, and so does the priest.'

'The hospital chaplain?'

'No. The Reverend Hildibrandur.'

I stare at Lísa Björk. I'm astonished.

'Yes, and there was one thing that struck me.'

'How so?'

Lísa Björk smiles again, as if she has more secrets to tell.

'What?'

'My friend said that she particularly recalled one visitor who came to see Dagrún just before Christmas, accompanied by the Reverend Hildibrandur.'

'Who?'

'Benedikt Björgúlfsson.'

'Wow.'

'That calls for a whole new set of questions about the priest's role in this tragedy.'

'My darling, you're a total genius.'

It takes me a while to digest this new information, and to mull over how this adds up as part of my preferred theory at the moment – that the murders of Benedikt and Bjarni are revenge for the fatal accident by the Thingvellir Lake.

Did the Reverend Hildibrandur make regular visits to Dagrún simply because, one way or another, he bore responsibility for the death of her husband, and for leaving her disabled? Did he see these visits as part of his Christian duty of penance and redress?

It's a possibility.

But that could hardly be the case for Benedikt Björgúlfsson. He certainly wasn't known for his sympathy, remorse or regret.

So why was he there at Dagrún's deathbed, just a few weeks before he himself was murdered?

There's only one man who has the answer.

55

The Reverend Hildibrandur is taking a class in the university chapel.

He watches from the front pew as budding theologists serve at the altar. They're giving repentant sinners the opportunity to taste the consecrated bread and wine, the flesh and blood of the Redeemer. All under a pale blue fake sky.

Back in ancient times this odd ceremony convinced Romans that Christians feasted on the flesh and blood of babies. But that was before the Emperor Constantine figured out that the Christian church could be good business in political terms.

I take a seat at the back of the chapel. I can wait for the class to come to an end.

When my phone rings, I step out into the corridor.

'I want you to know that the court ruling took us just as much by surprise,' says Gunnbjörn Hannesson, not bothering with a greeting.

'What prompted the judge to reach this insane decision?'

'Glúmur's lawyer presented written statements by the two Lithuanians at Efstakot, taking full responsibility for both keeping Ilona captive and running the speed factory. Both of them denied ever having had any contact with Glúmur related to these offences.'

'All of which is obviously false,' I snap. 'And completely contradicts Ilona's and Svanhvít's testimony, and presumably Robertas's statements as well.'

'I know that. We're already taking an appeal to the High Court.'

The servant of the Lord doesn't want to talk to me once his class has finished.

'I would ask you to be so kind as to leave me in peace for the moment,' he says.

'No problem,' I say. 'Just as soon as you've explained to me why you've been a regular visitor at the bedside of Dagrún Sveinsdóttir.'

'One of the tasks we perform is to serve the sick.'

'And why you took Benedikt Björgúlfsson with you on one such visit just two weeks before he was murdered?'

The Reverend Hildibrandur gives me a wan smile.

'I've underestimated you. You're a more dedicated seeker of the truth than I had expected.'

'Do you want to talk here?'

He shakes his head.

'I presume you're driving?' he says.

'Of course.'

'Then it would be timely to go home.'

The man of God sits silently in the passenger seat until we're hurtling along Miklabraut.

'I bought myself a beautiful car three years ago,' he says suddenly.

'What sort?'

'A Volvo jeep. But I no longer have it. In fact, I never actually owned it. It was purchased with foreign currency loans. They took it off me before Christmas when I could no longer meet the payments.'

'I see.'

'But it no longer matters to me,' he continues. 'I had forgotten for a moment that the scriptures tell us that wealth is transitory.'

'Your friends certainly weren't of that opinion.'

'I also had other opinions when I was younger, as did Saint Augustine, the sinner who gave himself up to the Lord's power and became a man of God.'

'I'm always dubious about holy men,' I say. 'I always have the suspicion that they have a band of propaganda merchants on their side, ready to lie for them.'

Hildibrandur gives me directions.

We drive eastwards along Breiðholtsbraut. Then we turn on to Vatnsendavegur where new residential districts sprouted like mushrooms during the greed years. That was before the house of cards of the Icelandic banking system came crashing down.

The servant of the Lord lives on Afturhvarf, in a magnificent new detached house.

There's a fabulous view.

Snow-clad mountain slopes rise beyond Elliðavatn, the lake's surface partly frozen over in the winter frost. That's Esja, the emblem of Reykjavík. There's the Hengillinn geothermal area that supplies most of the city's homes with hot water from the bowels of the earth, and the Bláfjöll ski slopes.

'I was also captivated by beauty, before coming to the conclusion that it's just another illusion,' the priest says as he opens the front door.

'I always feel better right away when I see something beautiful.'

'All the same, this is an illusion.'

He invites me into the living room.

I go straight to the big window to admire the encircling mountains. That's why I don't notice right away that the room is practically empty.

There's an old oak cabinet by the wall directly opposite the window. Some green cushions lie in a circle in the middle of the floor.

That's all there is in the living room.

The Reverend Hildibrandur sits on one of the cushions,

legs crossed. He bows his head, as if meditating – or praying.

'Please,' he says at last. 'Take a seat.'

I sit on the floor facing him.

'You have something against armchairs?'

'I couldn't keep up with the payments for the furniture,' he says. 'Any more than I could for the car.'

'You came out of the crash badly?'

'Back when we celebrated graduation from the faculty of law, in our eyes there were simple and obvious goals ahead of us. We wanted to be rich and influential, and quickly,' the servant of the Lord replies. 'At that night's feast Gunnar Kjartan told us that within ten years we would have all the power we could want in Iceland's society. That was the straight road ahead of my colleagues, while for many years I didn't think about money. For a variety of reasons, that changed around the turn of the century. That was when I followed the advice of my friends, invested in shares in banks and funds, was rewarded with a healthy return for some years, and bought this house with foreign currency loans, along with the new car and everything else that I might need to satisfy the imaginary demands of the time. But nobody mentioned to me that the banks were built on sand, so I lost everything in the financial crash. Today I have nothing but debts.'

'What was it that sparked this new interest in money?'

A sad smile crosses his face.

'I was caught up in what since the dawn of time has caused middle-aged men to make fools of themselves,' he replies. 'I fell in love.'

'Not for the first time, surely?'

'Yes. For the very first time I was captivated by the love of a woman.'

'Who is she?'

'That's of no account at this moment. But for some years love outweighed everything in my life, even the sin that has been my burden for so long. I wanted to do everything for my love. Subsequently I realised that this tumultuous, earthly passion was nothing but another ordeal on the path to God.'

'How?'

'You do not become closer to the Lord by amassing money or magnificent houses or other earthly chattels. Those lead to Satan.'

'I don't have much of an opinion of either of those guys.'

'Yes. I know that. There is no faith in your heart.'

'But I have an interest in justice. That means justice for my client, who is accused of a murder there's no chance he committed.'

'God also requires justice. A life for a life. An eye for an eye. A tooth for a tooth.'

'Tell me why you took Benedikt Björgúlfsson to meet Dagrún Sveinsdóttir.'

'Benedikt could sense death catching up with him,' Hildibrandur replies. 'He was already terminally ill and had no more than a few months to live.'

'You're telling me that Benedikt was already a dead man walking when he was murdered?'

'Yes, Ironic, isn't it? Benedikt had always been a strong man who rarely needed to see a doctor. For that reason he couldn't see this death sentence as anything other than for a life of sin, without God. In his anguish, he sought me out, and I encouraged him to look back and to experience our shared sin in the same way that I did a quarter of a century ago.'

'You mean the fatal accident on Grafninginn road in June 1983?'

The Reverend Hildibrandur looks up.

'You know?'

I nod.

'It's a relief that the seeker for the truth is coming to the end of the trail. Because I need to rest.'

56

The servant of the Lord gets to his feet. He goes over to the big window.

'I have a gift for you,' he says. 'It's in my tower.'

This turns out to be a square construction in the garden, facing the house. It occupies barely four square metres of ground, but it's probably five or six metres high.

The tower is topped by a glass cupola.

Hildibrandur opens a door that leads straight into the garden.

I follow him into the tower, clamber behind him up a steep aluminium ladder. I stand under the glass dome and admire the magnificent landscape.

'And see, I'll give you this...' he says, handing me a brown envelope that lies on a wooden bench in the middle of the glass house, and he takes a seat. 'Gunnar Kjartan never throws away anything he thinks might come in useful one day,' Hildibrandur says.

'What's this?' I ask, sitting next to him.

'Justice for that unfortunate boy and his girlfriend at Bessastaðir.' He smiled fleetingly. 'You accused me in the house of God of having the imprisonment of your client on my conscience, but that won't be the case if my suspicions are correct.'

'If...?'

'Last night Gunnar Kjartan invited me to have a drink with him, in memory of those who are no longer here, and during the night he began to let things fall, as we have always listened to each other's woes. But he doesn't have the head for drink he used to have, and fell asleep in the rocking chair. I've known for a long time where his darkest secrets are kept, and found what I was looking for.'

'I can hardly believe you found justice in some secret hiding place of Gunnar Kjartan's.'

The man of God doesn't let my sarcasm trouble him.

'Gunnar Kjartan offered to buy my house from the bank and then sell it back to me for one króna.'

'No doubt he can afford it.'

'Yes, but it's too late to turn back the clock. Love is gone. Dead, disappeared, a tale of tragedy...'

He gazes out over the snow-capped peaks to landward.

'I was going to tell you a parable of four young men who were celebrating a crucial turning point in their lives. They were reckless, and caused death and devastation. Not by intention, far from it, but what do the reasons matter to the outcome?'

'Dagrún was right.'

'After the collision, the young men scramble down to the edge of the Thingvellir lake in the darkness and look into the eyes of those who are suffering, without offering them a helping hand.'

'You looked into the eyes of Dagrún and Tómas there in the wreckage?'

'This awful event causes one of the young men unbearable anguish, but barely affects the other three, no more than if they had hit a bird or a fly. They think only of saving their own skins, and that's what happens.'

'Yes, for a quarter of a century. So what changed during last winter?'

'The world crumbled again.'

'What do you mean?'

'Trinkets, nothing but trinkets, but I forgot and allowed *Morgunblaðið* to print the picture that was taken of us out celebrating in the summer of 1983. When Dagrún saw the picture, all those horrific memories came flooding back, of the faces she had chosen to forget.'

'I see.'

'Tómasína was with her mother, she showed her the newspaper, because she took pride in knowing me. How was I to answer her questions?'

'Doesn't the truth redeem you?'

'The truth demanded more courage than I could muster at that moment. I regret that I had not long ago entrusted Tómasína with the secret of my inner anguish. The sin is mine, and mine alone, because I should have borne witness that terrible night but both my courage and my manhood were found wanting.'

'It's never too late to tell the truth.'

'It is too late. I have lost her.'

'Tómasína? You mean...?'

'Yes. She twice changed my life. That was first when she said she loved me, and then when the realisation hit her of how dreadfully I had deceived her.'

'So you're Sveinfríður's Rock?'

'It's God's will that even the mightiest rocks are made of sand.'

'Did that spur her on to seek revenge?'

The Reverend Hildibrandur shakes his head.

'It was not vengeance that brought about the deaths of my friends.'

'And the threatening cards?'

'Those I bought on the internet.'

'You?'

'They served to kindle the flame of fear.'

'The flame of fear?'

'It was fear that hastened their end.'

'Fear?'

'Benedikt feared death, terrified that his past would be too heavy a burden in the eyes of the Lord. The fear of death changed my friend, awakening a conscience that had lain dormant in his heart since boyhood.'

'You mean he was redeemed?'

'Benedikt wanted to use the months left to him to atone for his misdeeds. I took him to Dagrún's sick bed so that he could beg forgiveness. He knew she couldn't hear a word he said, but I convinced him that God hears everything and for that reason it was important to confess all his sins.'

'All of them?'

'Yes. Benedikt invited us, his friends, to a dinner between Christmas and New Year. He told us that he was writing a comprehensive confession of all his misdeeds throughout his life, both his personal life and in business, and he hoped to finish that work in the few months he had left. Such a confession would be the only way for him to be at peace with himself before death and to obtain forgiveness when facing God. I welcomed my friend's change of heart, but Gunnar Kjartan and Bjarni reacted badly, and tried to convince him of the insanity of all this, not just for Benedikt's reputation, but also for his closest friends and colleagues. But Benedikt would not be moved, wanted to confess everything, and things turned out the way they did.'

'So who murdered him?' I ask. 'If it wasn't Sveinfríður?'

'Wait here a moment and whatever happens, look after that package,' the man of God says. 'I have more to show you.'

He clambers slowly down the aluminium steps.

I get to my feet, the envelope in my hand. I get to admire the snow-sided mountains in the distance. Until I hear an unexpected noise behind me.

Hell!

The Reverend Hildibrandur has pulled away the steps. I'm left up here in his tower.

On my knees, I look down through the opening. I see

right away there's no chance of getting down without the ladder.

I'm a prisoner in the tower of the servant of the Lord.

57

'That's your ringside seat where you get to watch the end of the Icelandic dream,' the Reverend Hildibrandur says.

The end?

Has this guy completely lost his mind?

I fish my phone from the pocket of my red-brown leather jacket. I call Lísa Björk and ask her to get herself up here, to rescue me from this unexpected imprisonment by the man of God.

He takes slow steps back to the living room. He pauses there for a moment. Then he opens the large oak cupboard. He takes out three plastic cans. He takes one over to the door, and pours liquid over the floor.

What's he up to? Wrecking the new parquet in the living room?

Hildibrandur throws the empty can aside, and fetches the next. He pours the contents out in front of the oak cupboard.

The servant of the Lord uses the third can to soak the cushions that lie on the floor. The he lifts the can high over his head, and the liquid cascades over him.

This is truly disturbing.

His clothes are soaked. And it's definitely not water.

I call the emergency line. It's not easy to stay calm as I give them the address, and ask for an ambulance and the fire service right away.

'Has the fire taken hold?'

'Just send them up here this fucking minute!'

The man of God has taken a seat on one of the cushions.

With his left hand he lifts a tiny silver cross to his lips. Then his gaze moves to the window. He looks to the heavens.

'Nearer, my God, to Thee!' he calls out.

At the same moment, the Reverend Hildibrandur is enveloped in a blinding burst of flame, which spreads through the room with terrifying speed.

I watch this dreadful pyre with horror. Although I wish I could, I can't look away.

This magnificent new house is in flames by the time the fire trucks screen to a halt, sirens howling.

A moment later, Lísa Björk comes running into the garden. She stares dumbstruck at the burning pyre. She clearly thinks I'm inside.

I call her mobile and convince her that I'm in the tower, a prisoner under the glass dome.

She gets one of the firemen to help her put the aluminium ladder back in its place. I clamber down to solid ground, clutching the brown envelope.

'What happened?' she gasps.

'He set himself on fire in there.'

Lísa Björk shudders.

The fire chief comes running over. He roughly shepherds us away from the burning building. His team does its best to cope with the fire.

It's not long before the large windows of the living room shatter in the intense heat. Lethal shards of glass shower the firemen at work in the garden.

They don't venture inside until the fire is almost extinguished. There's nothing in there that can be saved. Just the charred remains of the deceased.

I entrust Lísa Björk with the brown envelope while I go to the station with the boys in black. I'm required to give them a statement explaining how the fire started. Later on

I ask her to drive me home in the silver steed to the red town house. I don't trust myself behind the wheel.

Slumped in the black boss chair, I allow myself a slug of Jack D, and then another. It's needed after that horrific sight.

But there's nothing that's going to erase the memory of that living firebrand.

'Why did he do it?' Lísa Björk asks.

It's beyond me why anyone would think to take their own life in such a horrific manner. All the same, I try to give her an answer.

'He said he'd lost everything. Except the connection with God.'

She's still holding the brown envelope.

'What's this?'

'Justice for my client, according to the deceased. I understand this is something he found at his friend Gunnar Kjartan's house.'

Lísa Björk rips it open, and extracts a black video cassette. She reads the note that's stuck to it.

'Well, now,' she says.

'What?'

'A recording from the security camera at Bessastaðir.'

'The recording that disappeared?'

'Let's hope so.'

I take my glass with me as I follow Lísa Björk to the meeting room.

She slips the tape into the old VHS player I've been meaning to take to the dump for years.

A coarse image of the church at Bessastaðir appears on the flatscreen. It shows the road next to it, and the parking lot. The time stamp is around 1300 on the 2nd of January.

'Fast-forward,' I say.

Sveinfríður appears first, parking her car by the church. She marches towards Bessastaðir, and is gone from the picture.

It's getting close to the time of the Presidential reception and more cars appear.

'There,' I say and Lísa Björk freezes the image. Sverrir Guðbjartsson can be seen opening the door of Sveinfríður's car.

'All right. Keep going.'

My client sits in the car. A minute later and he's asleep on the back seat. The top of his head is just visible.

At around four, two men walk along by the church, deep in discussion. Their backs are to the camera.

But there's no mistaking who they are, and I gasp. Of course it's no surprise to see Benedikt Björgúlfsson walking to the church. I had been expecting that. It's the man at his side who is the surprise. It's Gunnar Kjartan Vestmann.

Twenty minutes later, Gunnar Kjartan emerges from the church, alone.

'This is amazing,' Lísa Björk says.

He stops half-way, and makes a call. Then he continues towards Bessastaðir.

A little later the camera captures a young man striding towards the church. He disappears around a corner, and reappears at exactly 16.36.15.

'There!" I yell.

Lísa Björk freezes the image again.

We both stare at the grainy image of the young guy at the corner of the church with something in his hands. No doubt it's the candlesticks, wrapped in an altar cloth.

'Play.'

The guy goes over to Sveinfríður's car, places his burden in the boot, and shuts it carefully.

'Now.'

Again, Lísa Björk freezes the replay of the man planting the murder weapon in Sveinfríður's car. All the while, my client sleeps on the back seat.

It's Glúmur Aðalsteinsson.

58

Sunday 26th April

The majority of the people of Iceland have voted for a new direction in government. They want to see healthy reform in the wake of the banks' collapse.

Freyja Dögg is one of those who believes that a fresh Parliament is going to get a handle on the corrupt system of power and money, and that it's time to turn our backs on the insane partying and greed policies of the last few years.

When we meet on Austurstræti I don't bother airing my doubts. I don't see any need to put a damper on her infectious optimism.

Time can do that by itself.

She's heard nothing about her grandparents, Hjördís and Hákon. Sandra Ósk demanded absolute confidentiality concerning her parentage.

'I want that matter buried deep,' she said during the election campaign.

'Buried deep? How?'

'I never want to hear that family secret mentioned again.'

'And the inheritance from Hákon's estate?'

'It's out of the question to accept anything whatsoever from him. I know the truth of the matter, and that's enough for me. That should be enough for you as well, considering your client's dead.'

'I was asked to find Ásthildur and tell her the truth.'

'That's what you've done.'

'Understood. You're not curious to know more about Hjördís and Hákon?'

'No. They're nothing to do with my life.'

'I have a number of items of Hákon's,' I say. 'Including a letter to his daughter.'

'Shred it.'

'Really?'

'Yes. My decision is final. I will never again discuss this matter, with you or anyone else. This matter is closed.'

'It's entirely your decision.'

I have to admit that Sandra Ósk's attitude takes me by surprise. I imagined that everyone would have a sliver of curiosity about their real parentage, even wealthy politicians.

After thinking it over, I write a short letter to the Reykjavík District Commissioner. I explain my search for Ásthildur Ásvaldsdóttir, named in his will by Hákon Hákonarson as his daughter, has come to an end without anyone coming forward. Consequently, I will not continue to claim that she has to be his legal heir. So matters of inheritance can follow the usual process.

On the other hand, I decided to let Hákon's letter to his daughter remain unopened at the back of my filing cabinet for the time being, even though Sandra Ósk wanted it destroyed.

I suspect that one day she might change her mind, especially if she drops out of Parliament. In that case she'll no longer need to worry about image over truth.

The last few months have seen the bones of power given a healthy shake.

Lísa Björk and I were both present when the city's finest got their first opportunity to see the stolen footage from the security camera at Bessastaðir.

The jobsworths could hardly believe their own eyes. But they couldn't deny that the evidence was damning.

Then there was a burst of turmoil. Arrests, houses searched, people in custody at Litla-Hraun.

The media coverage was just completely mad at times. They also seemed to struggle as much as the cops with the thought that one of the country's most powerful men could have murdered his longstanding business partner. Maybe even two of his friends, if the boys in black can prove that he also finished off Bjarni Bjarnason.

There's no certainty of that. Gunnar Kjartan has a horde of lawyers at his beck and call, ones who know the system inside out, as they themselves are cogs in the wheels of power.

They've put every possible obstacle in the way of the blackbirds' investigation. Every single ruling by the District Court is appealed to the High Court. They've repeatedly tried to prevent a search of his house, and when that didn't work, they did their best to limit access to the stacks of documents the cops took away with them. That includes the laptop that Fat Raggi is certain belonged to Benedikt Björgúlfsson, although the boys in black still haven't managed to crack encrypted files.

So the wheels of justice have been turning with glacial slowness recently. Nobody has been charged with the murder, or with Ilona's kidnapping.

But they're both on remand, Gunnar Kjartan and Glúmur.

According to what Máki has heard, Gunnar Kjartan at first denied everything, adamant that Benedikt was alive when they parted in the church at Bessastaðir.

That doesn't tie up with Glúmur's testimony. The lad's clearly not prepared to take a sixteen-year rap on his uncle's behalf.

'I hear that Gunnar Kjartan's now claiming that he lashed out in self-defence,' the old newshound said. 'That

Benedikt turned on him, and he snatched up a candlestick to defend himself.'

I have no idea how Benedikt's murder came about. I have only a passing interest now that my client is a free man.

Sverrir Guðbjartsson is at a rehab clinic. There's a chance that this third attempt to shake off addiction will be more successful than the previous two.

But that's not my problem either.

Because we're on our way to the petting zoo.

I park the silver steed not far from the ice rink in Laugardalur. I look up, hoping it'll stay dry for the next hour or two.

'Seals! I want to see the seals!' Sóley Árdís yelps. 'Come on!'

The place is crowded today. Spring is in the air and the kids want to see the lambs and calves taking their first steps.

My daughter knows she's not supposed to run ahead of me. She fidgets with impatience on the pavement while I lock the car.

I let go of her hand when we get to the seals' enclosure, letting her admire them to her heart's desire. But I take the opportunity to scan the crowds for a familiar face.

'*Hæ*,' Rósalind says, from behind me.

I turn, and am instantly lost in those green eyes of hers.

Love's a strange bastard, as Mother said.